THE LOST RELIC

BY ERIC S BROWN

SEVEREDPRESS

THE LOST RELIC

Copyright © 2023 by Eric S Brown

WWW.SEVEREDPRESS.COM

ISBN: 978-1-922861-92-4

THE LOST RELIC

Storm clouds gathered in a mass of growing darkness beyond the Plexi-glass of the penthouse window. Dixon watched them with an intense fascination. His hands were clasped behind his back. He stood there mesmerized by the power of the cumulonimbus.

"Mister Than," a voice called.

Dixon Than turned to see that Mr. Adler, from the private military contractor firm he'd hired, had emerged from the elevator which connected his penthouse to the main building below. Adler, as always, came across as a bit flustered and on edge, palms running over the cloth of the expensive suit he wore, smoothing its fabric. His silver-rimmed glasses were pushed high upon his nose. It was all an act of course to put his clients at ease. He was an administrator and nothing more. That much was painfully obvious about him and exactly the image Adler was trying to project. Dixon knew better, of course. No one worked for the Colonel without seeing at least some time at the sharp end. Dixon preferred dealing with Colonel Bradick. The Colonel was a hard and steady man, the sort with whom one always knew exactly where they stood. . .and considering what Dixon was paying Moreau Inc. that was a good thing.

"Ah, Mr. Adler,"Dixon forced a wry smile. "I trust that all proceeds as planned."

He could already tell that it didn't. Dixon was very good at reading people, even those as strange as Mr. Adler.

Adler shook his head sadly. "I am afraid not Mr. Than. That's why I am here."

"Oh,"Dixon replied, giving Mr. Adler a chance to better explain.

"The three teams Colonel Ringo assembled for you are ready for immediate deployment, sir, but. . ."Adler shrugged. "We have been unable to locate the specialists you wanted brought in."

"What?"Dixon asked, the frustration he was feeling beginning to swell into something more akin to a raging fury. Dixon managed to keep himself from grabbing Mr. Adler by the throat and choking the little man until Adler turned blue.

"I can see that this is upsetting for you,"Mr. Adler stated the obvious. "But rest assured. . ."

"What is the problem?"Dixon asked. This time his voice was cold and rolled out of him like a low rumble.

"Let's just say that Dr. Phisher is very elusive, sir,"Mr. Adler admitted.

"That is simply unacceptable,"Dixon glared at the little man in front of him. "The operation can't proceed without him."

Adler balked at that. "Sir. I will have you know that our firm is the best in the business. We most certainly can handle. . ."

"No,"Dixon stopped him. "You can't. You'll find Phisher, bring him in, and assign him to the third team. However much it costs, whatever it takes, Phisher will be with your people when the teams are deployed. If he isn't, our business is concluded. You'll not see a penny from me. Do I make myself clear?"

"We have a contract,"Mr. Adler suddenly showed more backbone than likely anyone who hadn't seen through his act would think possible, straightening up to meet Dixon's eyes.

"Of which you'd be in breach,"Dixon stated with no emotion in his voice.

"You're being unreasonable,"Mr. Adler argued.

"That is merely your opinion,"Dixon cocked his head slightly sideways. "I'm quite sure the courts wouldn't agree with it."

"And what would you have us do, Mr. Than?"Mr. Adler snarled.

"I would have you locate Phisher and add him to the ^{third} team before deployment, as I paid you to do," Dixon reminded Adler as if the man were an idiot.

"Fine,"Adler growled. "We'll hold the teams until Phisher is located and brought in."

"Good, Dixon nodded, his anger having faded away like a wraith in the night. "Is there anything else?"

"No, Mr. Than, there isn't,"Mr. Adler was still fuming. "Though I will say I don't understand what's so important about one man, specialist or not."

Dixon laughed. "It's not your place to, Mr. Adler. Now go and bring me the relics I hired your people to obtain."

Adler disappeared into the elevator and left the penthouse. Dixon watched the little man go. Good help was hard to find. This was true. Still, the Colonel's people really were the best in their field. Adler hadn't lied about that.

Returning his attention to the weather outside, Dixon sighed. It had taken so long to figure out where the three pieces had been hidden away. . . so very long. He could wait another few days for them to be gathered and delivered to him. Regardless, there was no other choice. Dixon had done all he could. It was up to the Colonel's people at Moreau Inc. to complete the task at hand. Lightning flashed outside. A roll of thunder shook the glass of the window before Dixon in its frame. He smirked at the storm as if taunting it. Soon. . . soon the pieces would be in his hands at last.

****

Jason Phisher left work early, sneaking out the back of the bookstore. Lily would be ticked when she realized he was gone. It wouldn't be the first time or the last. Jason knew Lily wasn't going to fire him over it. He was too good at his job and she needed help too badly. Rain was falling. The sky was dark above the alley. Jason could feel them coming. Despite all his efforts to leave his old life behind, it was catching up to him.

Once he'd been a child prodigy, a genius, and a rising star in the realm of academia. By the age of twenty, Jason had doctorates in archaeology, history, and crypto-anthropology. His future was as bright as the stars on a clear summer night back then. Then the dreams started. At first, he had believed them to be just nightmares born of stress. Jason cut back on his writing for the journals, reduced his continuing studies slowing his progress towards the next Ph.Ds he was working on, and even canceled a lecture tour that summer. The dreams didn't stop though. With the passage of time, they only grew worse. His colleagues suggested seeing a therapist. Haunted as he was, Jason took their advice. The first therapist he saw was a woman named Martin. Jason saw her once a week. After two months, she killed herself. He was told it was because of problems in her marriage and at the time, Jason believed it. His second therapist, Dr. Page, after only a month of seeing him, was found in a bathtub full of bloody water, wrists slit to his elbows. Still, Jason hadn't understood what was happening until his third therapist, Dr. Henry. Ex-military, Dr. Henry was a big man and though in his forties, young enough to be tough as a fragging bull. Henry hadn't taken his own life like Martin and Page but came after him instead. Jason could vividly remember Dr. Henry's eyes that night. They were bloodshot and burning with a need to end him. Dr. Henry would have succeeded too except that Jason's gut warned him that something was off that evening. He had been sleeping with an ancient Celtic throwing knife from his collection of artifacts. The blade was clasped in a hand that was tucked under his pillow. Dr. Henry crashed through the locked door of Jason's bedroom like a raging bull, sending splinters of breaking wood flying. Lunging at him, Dr. Henry's huge hands had slammed down, gripping his shoulders. That was when their eyes met and Jason saw the man's fear and determination. Jason brought up his knife and slid it into the side of Dr. Henry's neck. Hot blood sprayed as the big man let loose of him and staggered backwards. Dr. Henry backed up into the wall of the bedroom and slid down it, crumpling onto the floor as he bled out. That was the end of Jason's attempts to even pretend there was any normalcy remaining in his life.

Jason resigned his position at the university where he was teaching, stopped his writing and touring, and dropped his own classes. His bank account was far from wanting. With the celebrity of his youth had came a fair amount of money. Never being one to indulge in excesses outside of an occasional rare relic or artifact for his collection, Jason had saved most of it. Now he used that money to drop away from the face of the earth. He left Europe behind, moving back to the States where he was born, choosing New York as his new home. In a city so large, Jason figured he could blend in and be lost among the masses. And he had, perhaps too well. Not daring to risk another attempt at therapy, the only means of getting sleep open to him was that of self-medicating. Alcohol was his starting point and from there he spiraled to more powerful drugs. His bank account bled out just as Dr. Henry had from the wounds his addictions inflicted upon it. Jason found himself alone with his nightmares on the streets. Only then, out of instinct-driven self-preservation, did he try to face his dreams head on. It was then he found God and the faith that gave him the strength to finally get things under control. The nightmares didn't stop, every night they came, but Jason no longer let them tear him apart.

The staff of the homeless shelter Jason frequented the most helped him get back on his feet. Having quit the drinking and drugs, at the ripe old age of twenty-six, Jason started his life over, finding work first as a bag boy at a grocery store, then a dishwasher, and eventually worked his way up to where he was now, employed as an expert and cataloger at Lily's Rare Occult Books.

Many times during what Jason referred to as his"lost years"the city streets had tried to take his life from him. Muggers, drug deals gone bad, junkies on a trip that sent them out for blood, and everything else the world could throw at him had come his way. Always though, always, Jason had known when those things were going to happen and sometimes even saw in his mind exactly how they would play out. That strange ability he couldn't explain saved his life time and time again. When he woke up this morning, Jason could feel that something was off with the day. It wouldn't be just another day spent teasing Lily about her poor taste in books or haggling with whatever rich kid who stopped at her shop looking for the answer to all his problems in a supposed tome of spells and rituals that was written centuries or more before they'd been born. No. Today was different. Someone was out there, hunting for him, searching for him with such great desperation that Jason could feel it in his bones. His gut told Jason that if someone wanted him that badly it couldn't be for anything good. That was why he'd ducked out of work early and was standing in the rain like an idiot trying to figure out where to go. Whoever was after him, he sensed, was close enough to finding him that heading for his tiny apartment up the street was likely a very bad idea.

Lily was his only friend and though the two of

them weren't overly close outside of work, Jason couldn't turn to her for help. Doing so would only put Lily at risk too if whoever was out there sought him with intentions less than good and though he didn't know for sure, his past experiences had taught him that something bad lay ahead in his not too distant future.

****

Corporal Wiggins glanced around the corner, peering down the alley through the rain, and then looked back at O'Hara. "You sure that's the guy? I thought he was supposed to be an egghead. He doesn't look like a nerd to me. A junkie, maybe."

"That's him,"O'Hara assured him. She'd seen Phisher through the bookstore's window before they got out of the van. He was a pale, thin man. Average height, a bit more in shape than was expected for the sort of fella he was supposed to be, with long, gray flecked, black hair that was tied into a ponytail. The gray was odd because he didn't look old enough to have it. Phisher made her think of Geddy Lee, though he was somewhat better looking. It wasn't Phisher's appearance that concerned her. She'd pegged him for who he was right off. What bothered her was that Phisher darted out the rear of the store not long after they'd parked their van across from it. There was no way in hell the man should have known they were coming and even if somehow he had, there hadn't been anything to give away who they were. "I'll give you that something is off about him, though."

"Only one way out of the alley,"Corporal Wiggins smirked. "And that's through us."

O'Hara nodded. "Let's go in after him but keep it polite, Wiggins. Remember we need him in one piece and the guy's not done anything wrong."

"That we know of,"Wiggins snickered.

Together they walked into the alley, side by side, blocking off its exit. Phisher spotted them as soon as they entered. O'Hara noticed his eyes. They were scarlet. In them she saw fear and a fierce strength. She raised her hands, palms towards Phisher in a gesture of peace as the two of them approached him.

"Dr. Phisher,"O'Hara said, with no doubt in her voice as to who he was. "We're not looking for trouble. We just want to talk."

Phisher looked them over as if sizing them up. "What do you want from me?"

"We're here to offer you a job, Dr. Phisher,"O'Hara explained, doing her best to manage a friendly smile despite the tension of the situation.

"I have a job,"Phisher told her. "So if that's all, I'll kindly ask you to leave me alone and be on your way."

"You haven't even heard our offer, Doctor,"O'Hara countered.

"Stop calling me that,"Phisher snapped. "I gave up that life a long time ago."

O'Hara glanced at Wiggins. He just shrugged, as confused looking as she felt. What the hell did Phisher mean by that? she wondered.

"Hey man, we're not cops if that's what you're worried about,"Wiggins snorted.

"I didn't think that you were. Now if you'll excuse me,"Phisher said and walked towards them, heading for the alley's exit.

Neither she nor Wiggins moved from his path. Phisher stopped just short of them. She heard him sigh.

"Does it have to be this way?"Phisher asked, frowning.

"We've orders to bring you in, Doc,"Wiggins huffed. "One way or another."

The Corporal cracked his knuckles loudly.

Phisher ignored Wiggins and started moving again as if he was going to try to shove through him. Wiggins didn't give the good doctor the chance. He took a step forward, meeting Phisher, and reached out to grab him. O'Hara's mouth fell open in shock as Phisher caught Wiggins' extended limb perfectly and delivered a punch to the Corporal's throat before the Corporal could even so much as blink. Wiggins stumbled away from Phisher. The doctor took off at a full out sprint past him. O'Hara leaped into action, knowing that if they didn't get their hands on Phisher right now they might never get the chance again.

O'Hara's booted foot swept through the air at

Phisher's head as he neared her. Her high kick was an instinctual action meant to stop Phisher in his tracks. It should have been impossible for him to see it coming and yet the doctor bent backwards, getting his head just out of the way of her foot. Still, the attack forced him to stop so O'Hara engaged him, springing forward. She let loose a flurry of blows aimed at his stomach and face. Phisher parried each of them perfectly as if he were utterly in tune with her very soul. O'Hara's eyes were wide. She dropped, sweeping a leg out in an attempt to at least take Phisher down, off his feet. She could tell Phisher knew that was going to be her next move but there was no time for him to counter it. She was faster than he was and that made the difference. Phisher toppled, grunting as he splashed into the water that was forming puddles in the alley. O'Hara threw herself atop him, punching downward at his forehead. Phisher jerked his head to the left in the nick of time and her fist struck the pavement. She gritted her teeth against the pain in her knuckles and brought her hand back up. Phisher was squirming under her, trying to get free. He likely would have, too, except that Wiggins came running to them and kicked Phisher in the top of his head. Phisher went limp, knocked unconscious.

"Frag, Wiggins!"O'Hara yelled. "Did you have to be so rough?"

"Rough?"Wiggins growled. "That pale bastard

nearly killed me!"

O'Hara shook her head. "Stop being a baby and let's get some cuffs on him."

"Damn straight,"Wiggins rolled Phisher over, slapping them on, as O'Hara got to her feet. "I sure didn't fragging see that coming. I mean, where does a guy like this loser learn to fight like that?"

O'Hara didn't have an answer.

"And did you see his eyes?"Wiggins went on. "They were freaky as hell."

"Eyes like his aren't unheard of. They're just rare,"O'Hara commented.

"I ain't never seen anything like them before,"Wiggins grunted. "Creepy as hell, if you ask me."

****

Jason came awake with a start. Sitting in a chair, he tried to leap out of it. His arms were handcuffed behind it though and he couldn't. Jason's head swept around, taking in his surroundings. He was clearly in some sort of interrogation room. His head ached. Jason didn't remember what happened to it, only that he had been wrestling with a strange lady who was one hell of a fighter. His ability to sense trouble that was coming his way had never failed him before. This was a first. It was almost unbelievable. There had only been two people against him and neither had drawn a weapon. He had faced odds a lot worse than those before and came out on top due to his curse. Others might have called it a gift but Jason didn't see it like that. It was just part of the nightmares that plagued him or maybe a side effect of them. Jason had been cuffed before and gotten free. There were a lot of tricks up his sleeves. Before he could try though, the door to the interrogation room opened.

The woman he had fought with and a man Jason didn't know walked in together. The man wore the rank of a colonel on his chest though it wasn't exactly a uniform he wore At least not one from any branch of the service that Jason recognized.

"Glad to see you awake,"the woman smiled at him. "We had you checked out for a concussion, or worse, when we brought you in. There were no signs of anything serious."

"Just who the hell are you people?"Jason gawked at them.

"I'm Lieutenant O'Hara,"the woman answered. "And this is my C.O., Colonel Ringo."

"You're military?"Jason didn't believe that.

"No,"O'Hara shook her head, her shoulder length red hair swaying. "We're private contractors."

"Like Blackwater?" Jason looked both of them over again.

O'Hara shook her head again. "They're called Constellis now I think but no, not like them. We're better."

"Moreau Inc,"the Colonel spoke. His voice was

deep and stern. "And we were hired to bring in some relics that our employer says you're the world's leading expert on. In fact, he insists that one of them is unattainable without you."

"So you just kidnapped me off the street?"Jason fumed. "You can't do that. I'm an American citizen. I've got rights."

O'Hara looked to the Colonel but he just laughed.

"Son, you dropped off the grid a long time ago,"Colonel Ringo grinned. "You've been changing your name and identity ever since then. No one even knows the real you is still alive, much less where you are."

Jason couldn't argue that. The Colonel was spot on in his estimate of the situation. Moreau Inc. could do whatever they wanted to with him and no one would ever know or care.

"Besides, the lieutenant here was only trying to offer you a job,"Colonel Ringo's grin had became a wry smirk. "You're the one who came at them. They only did what they needed to restrain you."

"That's one way of looking at things I suppose,"Jason admitted.

"Regardless, Dr. Phisher, you're in our custody now and the job offer remains on the table,"the Colonel told him.

"And this is the part where you offer me an obscene amount of cash for my help, isn't it?"Jason quipped.

"I would if I thought that would work,"the Colonel nodded. "But I've known men like you before. . ."

Jason stopped him there. "No, sir. I can assure you that you haven't."

"What I am offering you, son, is a place to fit in. O'Hara and Wiggins both say you're one hell of a fighter. My employer seems to think you're a lot more than what you seem, too. I know you're clean now and off the drugs that once ruled your life. Moreau Inc. can be a place that can not only offer you a purpose again but perhaps a sort of family too. No more running. No more hiding. A home, son, that's what I am offering you,"the Colonel finished.

Blinking, stunned, Jason had no idea what to say. Either the Colonel could read people better than most others Jason had ever met or was making a guess at what he wanted based on the intel Moreau Inc. had gathered on him.

"What makes you think that's what I want?"Jason asked.

"Aren't those the things everyone wants?"the Colonel countered carefully. "There would be money too, of course, a necessary evil in life. I can add nine grand a mission for starters, though if you live here at our corporate building, room and board would be free. You'd make more as you get more training too, though I know the money isn't really a factor."

Jason met the Colonel's eyes with his own. "And what exactly do I have to do to join your organization?"

"Help us get our hands on this,"the Colonel took a folder out of his jacket and slid it across the table.

"I can't exactly open that now, can I?"Jason frowned.

"O'Hara,"the Colonel barked.

She got up and moved to come around behind Jason, taking the cuffs that bound him off.

Jason didn't hurry to reach for the folder. He looked at Colonel Ringo instead. "So you're telling me your firm was basically hired to be Indiana Jones?"

The Colonel gave a real laugh. "Something like that, I suppose. It is a bit out of our normal wheelhouse but the money is too good for anyone but a fool to pass up."

Placing the tips of his fingers on the folder, Jason dragged it across the table to him. He rubbed at his raw wrists where the cuffs hadn't been kind to them before picking it up. As he did, a wave of dread washed over him, making Jason shudder.

"You okay?"O'Hara asked, moving back around to where he could see her. She stood behind Colonel Ringo.

"I'm fine,"Jason lied. He really wasn't. The folder in his hand felt as if it weighed a ton. A part of him wanted to throw it back at the Colonel, right into Ringo's face. Jason knew just how stupid a thing to do that would be so instead, he slowly opened the folder. Inside was a picture of what looked to be a piece of obsidian. Black as midnight, the piece was obviously part of a whole, something that was delicate and now shattered. Jason felt as if he should recognize the piece but couldn't place what it was. Even so, looking at it made him feel sick.

"That is what we're after,"O'Hara told him. "Pretty damn ugly I know but supposedly it's worth billions."

Jason believed her. There was quite a market and black market for artifacts lost to time. He owned a few himself but nothing ever on the level this shard had to be.

"Our employer must have it,"Colonel Ringo said, reaching into the other side of his vest to produce a cigar. He lit it with a lighter from the pocket of his pants, inhaling deeply.

Already feeling queasy, the sweet but acidic smell of the smoke nearly made Jason vomit.

"Those things will kill you,"Jason rasped.

"A lot of things will, son,"Colonel Ringo agreed,"But nothing has taken me down yet."

"Do you mind. . ."Jason started.

"I do,"Colonel Ringo scowled and took another puff from the cigar.

"Right then." Jason forced himself to look at the

picture again.

"Do you know what it is?"Lieutenant O'Hara asked.

Jason shrugged. "It could be a lot of things. This is just a shard of a singular piece. Hard to tell much from just this."

"A shard,"Colonel Ringo repeated the word. "That explains why we're being sent in three different directions at once."

"What?" Jason glanced at O'Hara.

"Our employer is sending us out to three separate locations. A piece like that is supposed to be located at each of them,"she informed him.

"Why hire a para-military group?"Jason shook his head. "I mean, that doesn't make much sense, does it?"

"That's what we thought too,"O'Hara answered honestly. "Most of us still think it."

"One of the pieces is in a war zone, son." Colonel Ringo exhaled smoke through his nose.

"And the other two?" Jason lowered the picture and set it on the table.

"He believes they're guarded by monsters,"O'Hara couldn't help but smirk as she said those words.

"You can't be serious,"Jason stared at the Colonel.

"Doesn't matter what I think,"Colonel Ringo shrugged. "If there are monsters, we frag them like we would anyone else in our way. If not, then the job is a milk run and everyone walks away happy."

Colonel Ringo ground out the end of his cigar on the table and then leaned over, putting his face close to Jason's. "What I want to know is why you're so fragging important if you don't even know what that thing in the picture is?"

"How the devil would I know?"Jason exclaimed. "You're the folks who kidnapped me, remember? I suggest you ask your employer why."

Colonel Ringo grunted and stood upright again, towering over Jason. "Regardless, son, you going along with us is part of our contract. So the question is, are you joining up or are we taking you along the hard way?"

Jason swallowed. He knew the Colonel wasn't fragging around. They would be taking him along no matter what. He thought about the insanity of it all for a moment. His life had been strange enough so far. Given his present circumstances, joining up with Moreau Inc. actually sounded appealing to him. And Colonel Ringo had read him right in terms of needing a purpose in his life. Working at Lily's bookstore was fun at times and mostly paid the bills but Jason knew deep down he'd been longing for something more out of life, like he had spent all his years on the planet so far just waiting for something like this to come along. Besides, if these people got him killed, at least the nightmares would be over. . . and it wasn't as if he really had a choice anyway.

"Sure,"Jason nodded firmly. "I'm in. Sign me up."

****

Happy with Jason's agreement to join his organization, Colonel Ringo had left him with O'Hara.

"What do you say we get you settled in?"she offered. "I imagine you could use some food."

Jason couldn't remember the last time he'd eaten. His stomach grumbled as he thought about it.

"Come on,"O'Hara urged him. "Let's grab a bite then we'll get your paperwork done and I'll show you to your quarters."

"Quarters?"Jason stammered.

"Yeah, the Colonel wasn't kidding about living here,"O'Hara assured him. "A lot of us do."

"Where's here?" Jason looked around as O'Hara led him out of the interrogation room.

"This is the Moreau Inc. corporate building,"she answered. "And your new home, if you want it."

"I. . .I'll need time to think about that,"Jason said. "I mean, I am joining up. I just don't know about living here. I have a place of my own."

"I've been to that thing that passes for an apartment you live in,"O'Hara turned up her nose. "I'm not sure someone could pay me enough to live there."

"You get paid to kill people, don't you?"Jason pointed out.

O'Hara stopped, turning to face him in the corridor. "Now look,"she stabbed her finger into his chest. It hurt. "We're not like Blackwater. We're mostly good people here and the work we do, it saves lives."

"But you still kill people,"Jason didn't budge.

"Of course but we kill the bad guys,"O'Hara's cheeks were flushed with anger.

"Who's to say who the bad guys are?"Jason pressed her. "The Colonel? Whoever hires you guys?"

"The Colonel picks the jobs we take very carefully, Dr. Phisher,"O'Hara swore. "We're a force for good in this world. You'll see."

"When you're not being some rich guy's errand boys and fetching lost relics for him?" Jason felt bad as soon as the words left his mouth. He had been pushing too hard and too far already. Only his strange extra sense saved his butt as O'Hara took a swing at him. Jason brought up his right arm just in time to block a blow that likely would have broken his nose and knocked him over onto his butt. Him blocking her strike only seemed to make O'Hara that much more angry.

"I'm sorry!"Jason blurted out before she could take another swing at him. "I was being an ass and I am sorry."

"Damn right you're an ass,"O'Hara spat.

"I am. I said so,"Jason kept his voice calm and level. "But keep in mind, you folks beat me up and kidnapped me. I woke up handcuffed to a chair, remember?"

O'Hara sighed and seemed to relax a bit. "Fair point."

****

After getting his paperwork dealt with and grabbing a bite in the building's communal mess, O'Hara took Jason to his quarters. She slid a card through the slot of its lock control. The door swooshed open and O'Hara handed the card to him.

"Don't lose that,"O'Hara warned. "It's a pain to get a replacement."

"I won't,"Jason nodded, taking what she told him to heart.

"We're headed out in the morning. Make sure you get some rest,"O'Hara said. "I'll see you then."

"Thanks for everything." Jason watched her walk away, disappearing around the corner of the corridor.

He turned his attention to the open doorway and entered his quarters. The door closed by itself behind him.

The room was rather spartan. There was a bed, a footlocker, an adjoining bathroom, a small desk in the corner with a chair beneath it and that was pretty much it. The walls were a bare gray, drab, and stale. Jason supposed it was meant to be that way and that if he really stayed on with Moreau Inc. that it would be his to do whatever with.

Jason hadn't been given the chance to bring anything with him beyond the clothes he was wearing along with his wallet and keys. He opened the locker at the foot of the bed to find a pair of matching uniforms and accompanying clothes inside it. They were identical in color and style to the ones everyone else who worked for the company wore. Taking out a set, Jason sat them on top of the footlocker after he closed it. He flinched as a wave of pain shot through his head. It still hurt like hell. Though the Colonel's people had checked him out for any serious injury and found nothing, that didn't mean getting kicked in the head left one feeling great. Jason took off his clothes, heading for the shower, and turning it on. When the water was warm, Jason stepped into it and let it flow over him. He stood there, lost in his thoughts. His whole world had somehow managed to get even crazier than it had been. After a while, Jason stepped out and dried off. Rest was what he needed but Jason didn't want to sleep. Usually his nightmares were worse when his life was in turmoil. Beyond that, this particular flare up of his extra sense felt different. There was no escaping going to bed, though. His body had been pushed to its limits and couldn't take much more. The day had been as draining emotionally and spiritually as it had to his body.

Flopping onto the bed, naked, Jason sprawled out on it. His eyes stared up at the plain, smooth ceiling above him. He fell asleep almost instantly despite himself. Leaving the real world behind for the world of dreams, Jason found himself standing in the center of a snow storm. No. It was more than a snow storm. It was like a blizzard on steroids. In his dream, Jason was still naked. The cold bit at his flesh. Clutching his arms about himself, Jason staggered against the wind, wondering where in the hell he was. There was white all around him, on the ground, in the air. . . Jason could barely see anything. Jason knew he had to find shelter and quickly, or freeze to death. A silhouette became visible through the snow as Jason squinted into the distance. It had the shape of a man.

"Hey!"Jason yelled, waving his arms over his head, trying to get the figure's attention. "I need help!"

The silhouette seemed to turn towards him. Jason was already running in its direction. He skidded to a halt, though, as it came into better view. The figure standing in the snow storm wasn't a man at all. It was too tall and the proportions of its body were all wrong. The thing's head was huge and its arms didn't end in hands like a man's would. Instead, in their place, were something more akin to pincers. The creature's eyes glowed a bright green as they fell upon him. The power of their gaze took Jason's breath away, somehow chilling him more than the cold of the air.

A chittering sound came from the creature as Jason stared at it with a mixture of outright fear and awe. The mandibles over its mouth clicked together rapidly. The chittering paused and then began again. It was as if the thing were trying to talk to him. There was nothing remotely human about the sounds coming from it. They reminded Jason of the noises an insect might make. Still, the creature had an overall human shape, standing on two legs, despite nearly everything else about it being different. Jason almost screamed like a terrified child as massive wings unfolded from the creature's back. Giving him a final chilling glance, the thing took flight, disappearing into the white of the storm.

Jason woke up screaming. His skin was soaked with sweat. He jumped up from the bed in his quarters, trying to run, crashing into a wall. Jason landed on his butt, grunting. Shaking his head to clear it, Jason began to realize where he was and that the nightmare was over. It had left him shaken and horrified. Like all his nightmares, it felt so very, very real. A few minutes passed before Jason was able to collect himself enough to get up off the floor. He stumbled back to his bed, collapsing onto its edge, placing his head in his hands. Jason didn't want to believe that there was any chance the monster in his nightmare was real. . .but he knew his dreams well enough to know that the thing likely was indeed real and out there, somewhere, waiting on him to come to it.

****

O'Hara showed up at his door at 3 AM. Jason was already up, still awake. The nightmare had disturbed him far too much to return to sleep. He'd spent his time re-showering and getting ready.

"I half expected to find you asleep,"O'Hara teased.

"I don't sleep much,"Jason shrugged.

"Okay,"O'Hara said, not pressing him about the solemn tone of his comment. "It's time to get moving. The Colonel wants you to come in for a special briefing before we head out."

Jason nodded his agreement, not that he had a choice. Besides, he had no idea where they were even going so it'd be a good idea to find out.

The two of them took the elevator to the top of the Moreau Inc. building. A helicopter was waiting there for them. The Colonel sat in its rear, headset on. He motioned for them to join him. O'Hara took a seat next to the Colonel while Jason sat across from them, his back to the pilot. Jason donned his own headset.

"Good morning, Dr. Phisher,"the Colonel

greeted him as the helicopter rose from the building, soaring away into the darkness of the pre-dawn sky. "Lieutenant O'Hara tells me you are one of us now."

After the mountain of paperwork he'd had to sign, from non-disclosure agreements to junk he didn't even understand, and that was saying a lot, Jason figured the company pretty much owned him at this point. Jason sighed and didn't bother to remind the Colonel that he hated being called"Dr."again.

"Where are we going?"Jason asked, changing the subject.

"The airport,"the Colonel answered with a wry grin.

Jason frowned, glancing over at O'Hara.

"All of us, Moreau Inc.'s field personnel will be rallying there,"O'Hara explained.

"Before breaking into three teams, each with their own destination,"Colonel Ringo added.

"You mentioned three locations before,"Jason commented.

"I did." The Colonel passed Jason a folder. "Take a look."

Jason flipped through its contents. There was info on locations in Africa, the rural south of the United States, and Antarctica. He shivered seeing that third location.

"Those are the places our employer swears we'll find the pieces of the relic he's after,"the Colonel told him. "He gave us detailed intel on how to reach each of them."

"Really?"Jason asked.

"Really,"O'Hara assured him. "Whether it's truly trustworthy or not, that remains to be seen."

"But the level of his intel isn't anywhere near as freaky as some of the other things the man has warned us about,"the Colonel huffed.

"Each of these locations is supposedly guarded,"O'Hara said.

"Guarded?"Jason gave her a questioning look. "I thought these relics were supposed to be lost."

"You're sharp, kid. Real quick on the uptake." The Colonel leaned forward, "That was my thought too, straight away."

"These things we're after. . ."O'Hara paused mid-sentence as if to make sure she picked the right words to say. "They're not supposed to be guarded by people."

"What the heck does that mean?"Jason blinked.

"Monsters,"Colonel Ringo said.

"Monsters? What? You can't be serious,"Jason shook his head. "That's insane."

"You're telling me, son,"the Colonel snorted. "I've been in this business a long time. I've seen a lot of terrible things in this world but I ain't never once run across anything out there worse than us human beings. We're the monsters. There ain't no boogeymen hiding in the shadows or winged horrors diving out of the sky."

"Our employer disagrees with both of you,"O'Hara cut in. "He's adamant that there are monsters guarding the relics we're after and that we need to be prepared for them. Of course, he didn't go into any detail about what the monsters waiting for us out there would be."

"No, I suppose he wouldn't have, would he?"Jason smirked and yet deep down inside he wondered if monsters were really such a far fetched thing given the things that he himself could do.

"Doesn't matter either way,"Colonel Ringo growled. "We're getting those relics and delivering them."

"The Sarge and his guys will be heading to North Carolina for the relic there. Lieutenant Taylor will be taking a team to Scarnova in Africa for the relic there. . ."O'Hara said.

"And we're going to Antarctica,"Jason concluded. He felt sick at his stomach remembering his nightmare from the night before.

"Yep,"O'Hara nodded. "That we are."

The pilot's voice cut into their conversation, addressing the Colonel. "We've arrived, sir. I'm bringing us in."

"Copy that,"Colonel Ringo nodded.

The helicopter landed at what appeared to be a small private airport. Jason figured the place belonged to Moreau Inc. and was used as their launching point for any missions that required travel outside of New York.

Even as their helicopter was landing, one of the three transport jets at the airport was in the process of taking off. Its engines roaring, the jet shot upwards into the sky. Based on its direction, Jason speculated that its destination was Africa. Looking at the other two jets, Jason noticed that they had VTOL capability too. A group of armed men and women in Moreau Inc. uniforms were finishing up boarding one of the other jets. He watched the group disappear into the VTOL jet and its cargo door rise up closed behind them.

Colonel Ringo flung the side door of their helicopter open once it was firmly on the ground. "Come on, son," he barked,"We've got work to get done." Flinging his headset into the seat he'd been in, the Colonel jumped out onto the tarmac.

The second VTOL took off, heading southward, as the Colonel headed for the third VTOL with Lieutenant O'Hara in his wake. Jason rushed to keep up with them.

****

Aboard the VTOL jet that was en route for Africa, William"The Sarge"Watkins sat in its rear with the soldiers under his command. He was reclining with his back against the wall. The Sarge always liked to make sure his back was covered. It just made him feel better. He looked around at those with him. There was Rogers, a burly little man with a dark beard, who was all muscle and as fierce as a wild animal when need be. Across from Rogers sat Artie. She was like a daughter to the Sarge in a lot of ways. He hadn't recruited her but Artie had impressed him from the very first time they went into action together. The lady was a killer to the bone. She could crack bones and frag bad guys with the best of them. Artie looked more like a supermodel than a soldier in terms of her figure and that caused some issues with a few of the single guys at Moreau Inc. The Sarge was keenly aware that Artie could handle them herself but had some words with them anyway. Most people in the company were scared of him and the Sarge enjoyed using that to his advantage when possible. The Sarge flinched, realizing in a sense he was checking her out right now himself. She turned to glance his way, short cropped red hair above dark green eyes. The Sarge gave her a thumbs up to let Artie know everything was okay and shifted his attention to Marcus and Lucas. The two of them were twin brothers. They were identical in every way except for their hair. Lucas had dyed his green while Marcus had dyed his purple. They sat playing games on their phones, side by side. Kids, the Sarge thought, shaking his head. Not that the twins were really kids. Both of them were pushing twenty-five and lived their lives on the sharp end.

The Sarge supposed they weren't such a bad

group of killers, the hint of a smile forming at the edges of his lips. That was good. The place they were going was fragged up and in the middle of a bloody civil war. While they wouldn't be heading into the capital or even any of the cities near it, the Sarge knew there would still be enough roaming groups of rebels and proper military folks that running into some of them was more likely than he wanted it to be. Really, all they needed to do was march from the LZ the Colonel picked out for them into the jungle to find their target and then get the hell out. The Sarge didn't want to think about all the things that could go wrong along the way but they all knew the risks that came along with the job and he was damned sure his people could handle whatever got thrown at them.

Getting up, the Sarge left the rear of the plane. He entered the pilot compartment where Sam and Vic were. Sam was the pilot, long brown hair spilling down her back, smiling as usual, as she worked her magic in the sky. Vic was her co-pilot on this run, and though he was qualified to fly the VTOL bird, he was nowhere near Sam's level of skill and talent. He was just her backup and an extra hand if Sam needed one, given that they were landing in a war zone. What he lacked as a pilot though, Vic made up for on the battlefield. He was among the best soldiers Moreau Inc. had in its employ.

Sam noticed him. "We're almost to the LZ, sir."

"No trouble yet,"Vic added.

"That's what I like to hear,"Sarge smiled at them. "E.T.A.?"

"Coming in in five, Sarge,"Sam said.

"Take us down easy, little lady,"Sarge teased and left the pilot compartment.

"Okay folks!"the Sarge bellowed. "It's about time to earn our pay. Get ready and gear up. Standard formation when that door back there opens."

The Sarge walked through the rear section to stand next to the door. When it went down, he planned to be the first out of it. He wasn't expecting the jet to take fire as it landed but one never knew when you were in a part of the world like they were now. He took one final look at his crew and then braced himself just in case the crap did hit the fan.

The VTOL touched down. The door fell open in front of the Sarge and he jumped through it, boots thudding onto the ground. The jet was in the center of a wide clearing. Surrounding the clearing on all sides was a dense jungle. The Sarge's eyes scanned the trees as he put some distance between himself and the door so the others could get out behind him. Artie went west with Marcus. Rogers went left with Lucas. Vic emerged to stand in the doorway as the Sarge faced north. The front end sensors and heavy weapons of the jet faced southward. There was no sign of any danger in their vicinity.

When he was sure the LZ was secure, the Sarge called out,"Alright people.   Form up on me. Rogers, you got point. Vic, I want you in the rear."

The group got moving as the jet's rear door closed. The Sarge wasn't thrilled with leaving Sam alone but knew that in reality she'd be safer than they would. The jet was locked up and heavily armored. If anything did happen, she could always take off.

The group marched into the jungle. The cave that was supposedly home to the relic they were after wasn't that far away if their intel was correct. It would take them an hour or two to reach it, Sarge guessed. He grunted. The whacko that had hired them honestly thought there were monsters protecting the relic. The Sarge didn't buy that at all. At best there might be something like the apes in Congo, feral and flesh eating, the Sarge could see that.   Still, even those things hadn't been monsters, just beasts.

The sun was setting and the shadows among the trees were going darker and deeper.   Suddenly, Rogers came to an abrupt stop, staring into the jungle ahead of him. The Sarge gestured for everyone else to hold their positions and then crept up to where Rogers stood.

"Sit rep,"the Sarge asked, keeping his voice low.

"Something's   not   right,   Sarge,"Rogers

whispered. "There's someone out there watching us but I can't catch a glimpse of them no matter what I do."

The Sarge knew whoever it might be had to be damn good to keep out of Rogers' sight. That meant they were either professionals, better than either the local army or rebels put in the field, or their whacko employer was right. Still not willing to believe in monsters, the Sarge said,"Stay frosty and keep moving."

Rogers nodded. The burly, little man barely made it a few yards before all hell broke loose.

Something huge and black streaked from the trees at the rear of the group. The Sarge saw the flash of claws as Vic cried out. Vic was a fast bastard or the attack would have torn open his throat. As it was, the claws ripped through the cloth of his uniform, raking his right arm instead. Rolling with the blow, Vic brought his UZI around to aim at the thing speeding away from him. He let loose a cacophony of gunfire as hot lead chased after the shape disappearing into the trees. Splinters of bark flew as bullets hammered into them. The Sarge couldn't tell if Vic hit his target or not though.

The Sarge's crew closed their ranks quickly, all of them aiming their weapons at the trees.

"What the hell was that?"Marcus asked, eyes wide.

"Anybody get a look at it?"The Sarge snapped.

No one answered.

From somewhere in the trees surrounding them came a thunderous roar. The sound of it made the Sarge think of a lion.

"Frag me,"the Sarge heard Rogers mutter.

"Everybody hold your ground,"the Sarge ordered. "If anything moves out there, blow the hell out of it."

The jungle was silent. Night continued to fall and the darkness seemed to grow deeper with each passing second among the trees.

The creature, whatever it was, the thing sure wasn't as hell a man, leapt from the trees at Lucas. The twin met it with his M4 blazing. Though shrieking in pain, the thing still landed on him. Lucas went down, toppling to the jungle floor, wrestling against the creature. They all saw it now. The thing had the basic build of a human but was covered in black hair. It made the Sarge think of a panther. Hell, that was what it looked like exactly except for the fact it had human aspects to its overall form.

Razor sharp teeth glistened wetly in its mouth as the thing went for Lucas' throat, claws sunk into his shoulders, keeping a firm grip on him. Its yellow eyes glowed as the creature overpowered Lucas' resistance and bit into the side of his neck.

No one had a clear shot at the creature with it on top of Lucas. Marcus wasn't about to just give up on his brother, though. He ran at the creature, smashing the butt of his M4 into the top of its head. The creature jerked away from Lucas, long strings of bloody flesh being torn from Lucas' neck in the process.

Marcus saw that there was no hope of saving his brother. "No! You bastard!"the twin raged, raising up his M4 to bring its butt down at the creature again. This time, the thing was way too fast for him, easily avoiding the blow. One of its clawed hands shot out to grab Marcus by his leg. Claws dug deep into the back of his knee as the creature gave a jerk that took Marcus from his feet. Marcus landed hard on his back as the creature pounced on him.

The creature's move finally gave the Sarge a clear shot. His shotgun thundered. The heavy slug it fired ripped into the thing's side. Squealing and shrieking, the monster dove away from Marcus, opening it up to Artie's line of fire too. Her M4 roared on full auto. The Sarge saw the creature take over half a dozen of the rounds she fired in its back. Its horrid screeching and squealing came to an end as the thing collapsed onto the jungle floor. It lay there twitching.

The Sarge rushed to the creature and fired another blast of his shotgun straight into the back of its skull. Bits of white bone, black fur, blood, and brain matter exploded into the night. The thing dang sure wasn't getting back up now. Glancing around, the Sarge saw Artie squatting next to Marcus, checking out how badly the twin was hurt. Rogers came over to stand next to him. The burly little man hadn't gotten off a shot at the monster. He was carrying a belt-fed mini-gun that had likely been a good thing in terms of avoiding friendly fire.

"What the frag is that thing, Sarge?"Rogers asked.

"A monster,"the Sarge answered simply. "A real life monster."

"Guess that nutjob who hired us isn't as crazy as we thought,"Rogers commented.

"Looks not to be,"the Sarge agreed, though he wasn't really listening to Rogers anymore.

"It's like the thing is part panther and part man,"Rogers droned on.

The Sarge's mind was racing. Against all logic, the thing, dead on the ground in front of them, was real. Their employer had warned them of monsters. Not a single creature but more than one. If there were more and they were as fast and deadly as this one, his crew was in some serious trouble. No one had really seen or heard the thing before it attacked. The only thing that had prepared them at all was Rogers' gut feeling that something wasn't right in this place. The big question of course was just how many more of these things were they dealing with?

"Sarge,"Artie got his attention. He turned to see her standing with Marcus. The twin stood staring at the corpse of his brother, arms hanging limply at his sides. The monster's claws had shredded the muscles of his shoulders and upper arms.

"Marcus can't even hold a weapon much less fire one, can he?"Rogers grunted.

"What about my brother?"Marcus said ignoring the talk about his own condition. "We can't just leave him here."

"We've got no choice on that, Marcus,"the Sarge told him. "It's gonna take everything we have just for the rest of us to get out of here alive."

"We should leave him here,"Rogers cut in.

"What?" Rage flashed in Marcus' eyes and despite not being able to use his arms, he took a step towards the burly, little man.

"I wasn't talking about your brother, Marcus,"Rogers stood his ground, ready for the twin to come at him.

"You bastard,"Marcus snarled.

The Sarge moved in between the two of them. "I hate to say it, Marcus, but Rogers is right. You're going to stay here with Lucas' body. We'll pick it and you up on our way back. Got it?"

Marcus was too stunned by the order to do anything but mumble,"Yes sir."

"Artie, get him a weapon in his hands and see if you can figure out a way for him to make use of it. Vic, you're staying with him,"the Sarge barked and continued on before Vic had a chance to complain.

"There could be more of these things,"he kicked the panther man's corpse,"watching us and just waiting for a good chance to come at us right now. We need to get moving. The sooner we get that relic and get the hell out here, the better."

"I can pump him full of painkillers,"Artie nodded. "That should let him fight back if he needs to."

Artie went to work helping Marcus.

"Got any idea how to deal with these things, Sarge?"Rogers asked.

"Yeah I do,"the Sarge said. "It may seem stupid but I think it'll work."

The Sarge found a piece of wood that he liked the feel of and took off his combat armor long enough to remove the shirt under it. Wrapping the shirt around the top of the piece of wood, he turned it into a torch after getting his armor back on.

Seeing what the Sarge was doing, Artie made her own torch too.

"Seriously?"Rogers half chuckled. "Torches?"

"No animal likes fire, Rogers, the Sarge said sternly. "It's our only shot at even remotely making these things think twice about attacking."

"Fair enough,"Rogers nodded.

Rogers' mini-gun required both of his hands to carry and use effectively. The Sarge and Artie could always drop their torches if they needed to use their M4s and couldn't fire one handed.

The trio left Vic and Marcus behind, moving

deeper into the jungle. They moved as quietly as possible but the Sarge suspected that didn't amount to a hill of beans. The creatures they were up against would likely hear them regardless. He figured the things could see better in the dark too. The damn things seemed to have just about every advantage and there wasn't a blasted thing they could do about it.

No other attacks came, though. They came into view of the cave mouth where the relic was supposed to be and Rogers, still on point, once again motioned for them to hold up. The Sarge and Artie flanked him, peering out of the trees at the small clearing between them and the cave mouth. The torches gave away their presence but the Sarge didn't care. What they faced now was hugely different than moving through a jungle in the dark, exposed on all sides. No, this was a situation he could seize control of and turn the tables on the monsters who were almost certainly surrounding them. A feral snarl formed on his lips as the Sarge placed his torch on the ground and unclipped a flash bang from his belt. Artie appeared to take note of what he was doing and followed his example.

"On three,"the Sarge whispered just loud enough for Artie and Rogers to hear him. "One. . . Two. . . Three!"

The Sarge and Artie tossed their flashbangs from the trees. Artie's landed in the clearing in front of the cave while the Sarge's landed just inside it. As the flashbangs detonated, the creatures who had been lurking in the shadows were exposed. They squealed, howling in pain from the light that burnt their eyes. The Sarge and his crew burst into the clearing, firing at the monsters. Rogers' mini-gun spun, hosing two of the monsters to their right. Their flesh was ripped from their bones as dozens upon dozens of rounds tore into them. The Sarge charged straight at a pair of the panther men stumbling out of the cave. His shotgun boomed. The head of the panther man directly in front of him blew apart in a shower of gore as the Sarge worked the shotgun's pump, chambering another round. The other panther man blocking his path did its best to leap at him, still blinded. The Sarge met it with a blast to its stomach that opened up the panther man's guts. They slid out of the creature like red-drenched, purple snakes, coiling in the grass at its feet even as the Sarge chambered a third round, firing again. He finished the monster with a heavy slug that splintered the center of its rib cage. The panther man was thrown backwards, thudding onto the ground. Artie got her vengeance on the monsters too. With the skill of a true professional, she fired short, well aimed bursts with her M4, taking down more of the panther men in rapid succession before they could even get close to her.

The battle was essentially over before it even

began. The Sarge's tactic of using the flashbangs had turned it into nothing short of a massacre. If there were any creatures left, which the Sarge doubted, the things had either fled or were hiding in the cave with no intentions of coming out. He laughed at the thought. All they needed to do was toss some more flashbangs in there and getting their hands on the relic would be a cake walk. . . and that's what they did.

The last three creatures hiding in the cave didn't stand a chance as Rogers' mini-gun cut them to pieces, literally sawing one of the things in two. Blood was splattered all over the cave's floor and walls as the Sarge passed Rogers, taking the lead, heading deeper into it. At the cave's rear was an eerie pedestal. All around it, there were piles of bones, human and animal alike, as if the panther men had left them as offerings to some unseen god. The stone of the pedestal was etched with bizarre designs, like a totem pole almost. They pictured a monster with wings and an antlike mandible over its mouth. Though the etchings were crude, they got their point across. Whatever the thing in the etchings was, clearly, you didn't want to mess with it or hell, even meet it.

The relic they were after sat atop the pedestal within easy reach. The Sarge started to snatch it up but Artie reached out a hand to stop him.

"Hold up, sir," she said, "It might be booby trapped."

"Like in Indiana Jones?"the Sarge snorted but saw that she was serious.

"I don't think so,"he said. "This isn't a fragging movie."

"Yeah? Didn't we just kill a bunch of monsters, Sarge?"Rogers challenged him. "You only see them in movies too."

The Sarge thought for a moment. "I don't think it's booby trapped and I'll tell you why. Those things, the panther men, I think they were the trap. This was a holy spot of sorts to them and they died, to the last one of them, protecting it. I don't think they would have defiled this place with a back up means of protecting whatever the heck this relic is."

Neither Artie nor Rogers had a counter argument to that. They stood watching as the Sarge slowly reached out and took hold of the piece of strange metal sitting atop the pedestal. Nothing happened as he lifted it. The cave was still and silent all around them.

"See?"the Sarge said, "I told you, nothing to worry about."

The Sarge shrugged off his backpack and placed the piece of metal inside of it. Slinging the pack back onto his shoulders, he worked at reloading his shotgun as the three of them walked out of the cave, this time with Artie in the lead.

No further danger awaited them outside either, only the bullet torn corpses of the panther men which were already beginning to stink in the hot, humid air.

Hurrying through the jungle with Rogers in the lead, the trio heard gunfire in the distance.

"Frag!"Rogers yelled and increased his pace. The Sarge strained to keep up with him. For a little guy, Rogers was fast as hell. Glancing over at Artie, the Sarge saw that she was keeping up without what appeared to be much effort. Maybe he was just getting old.

They charged out of the jungle, ready for action, only to see Vic standing over Marcus. The twin was slit open from groin to neck. A dead panther man with the hilt of a knife protruding from the side of his throat lay near the two of them. Vic had heard them coming and held the M4 he carried pointed in their direction.

"Hold up!"Rogers shouted. "It's us, man!"

Vic lowered the carbine. "About fragging time! Did you get it?"

Rogers nodded even as the Sarge answered,"Frag yeah we did."

"Then what the hell are we waiting for? Let's get out of here before any more of these panther things show up,"Vic snapped.

"You're preaching to the choir, brother,"Rogers laughed.

"What about their bodies?"Artie asked, gesturing at the twins.

The Sarge was torn. Leaving the twins to rot in

this jungle didn't sit well with him. It felt like a flat out betrayal. Still, they were on the clock and there was no certainty that more of the panther things wouldn't be coming. As much as he liked to tell himself they had gotten all of the things in their assault on the cave, there could very well be more of the creatures prowling about the jungle. He just couldn't put everyone still alive at risk trying to drag the bodies of the twins along with them.

"We have to leave them,"the Sarge said, frowning. "Ain't no other choice."

"But. . ."Artie started.

The Sarge cut her off. "Get moving, people! Now!"

The group made it to VTOL without incident. Sam ran her pre-flight checks as Vic slid into the co-pilot seat next to her. The Sarge stood watching them as in the rear of the jet, Vic, Rogers, and Artie got strapped into their seats.

Everyone was solemn. They hadn't lost anyone in a while but that streak had just ended. Both twins had met their end on this gig. They were all professionals and knew that death and loss were just part of the game but it still stung.

"Take us home,"the Sarge ordered Sam and Vic.

"Yes sir,"Sam gave him a nod.

The VTOL rose up from the ground, above the trees, and then shot westward through the sky.

****

Lieutenant Hammer and his crew were in the rear of the VTOL as it streaked southward towards North Carolina.

"Whooeee, boys!"Brad whooped. "We're going to kick us some monster arse!"

Hannah rolled her eyes. "Don't tell me you buy that crap about there being monsters guarding this piece of junk we're being sent to bring in."

"Let him have his fun,"Shannon said, running the fingers of his right hand through his blonde hair. "At least it's better than continuously hearing about his sex life."

"Sex fantasies you mean,"Deb corrected Shannon.

"Hey!"Brad snapped at Deb. "What the hell?"

"Just call 'em as I see 'em,"Deb grinned at Brad.

"So, Brad,"Lieutenant Hammer spoke up, putting an end to the banter. "Just what kind of monsters do you think we'll be seeing in those mountains of yours?"

"Ain't my mountains, sir,"Brad turned serious. "They don't belong to anyone."

"Everything belongs to someone,"Hammer corrected him.

"That's a rather negative view of the world, sir,"Brad countered.

"Are you intentionally avoiding the question I asked?"Hammer frowned.

"No sir. Not at all. I reckon' it's just hard to

say,"Brad matched the lieutenant's frown with one of his own. "We got all sorts of monsters in the south. We got the Beast of Bladenboro. It's sort of a cat-dog hybrid thing. We got mermaids in some backwoods rivers. We got ghosts, spooks, haints, the Moon Eyed People, and the Wampus. There were supposed to be some vampires around at various times in history. And most of all, we got Bigfoot. There are so many sightings of that guy, it's hard to believe there's not an army of them somewhere in the mountains just waiting to come out and kill us all."

"Is that so?"Hammer smirked. "And exactly how many of those have you seen with your own eyes?"

Brad hesitated before answering. "Well. . ."

"None,"Hammer finished for him. "That's your answer, isn't it? You haven't seen any of them yourself."

"That don't mean they ain't real,"Brad said firmly. "Why my grandfather. . ."

Lieutenant Hammer held up a hand, silencing Brad. "I didn't ask for stories, Brad. My point is that for all the stories and tall tales about these monsters none of them are real. They're just myths."

Brad looked as if he wanted to argue more but apparently knew better. It was easy to see that Lieutenant Hammer wasn't about to be convinced that monsters were real.

"You gotta wonder what the weirdo that hired us wants with these relics he's sending us after anyway,"Deb commented.

"As long as the check clears, I don't suppose it matters,"Lieutenant Hammer shrugged.

"Amen to that,"Shannon smiled.

"For what he's paying, they've got to be worth a hell of a lot,"Hannah said.

Lance, the VTOL's co-pilot, entered the rear of the plane. "Lieutenant, Matt sent me to tell you that we're approaching the LZ."

Lieutenant Hammer scowled at Lance. "Why didn't he just use the comm?"

"We're having systems issues, sir,"Lance answered. "Nothing serious, just some interference."

"Interference from what?"Shannon asked before Hammer could.

"Don't have a clue,"Lance admitted. "Like I said though, it's only messing with our comms and some minor systems. We'll have it sorted before you guys get back from your hike in the mountains. Count on it."

"Make sure you do,"Lieutenant Hammer ordered.

Lance nodded and headed back to the pilot compartment.

"That ain't exactly a good way to start things off,"Brad shook his head.

"He said it wasn't anything to worry about,"Deb

said, though it sounded like she was trying to reassure herself as much as she was Brad.

"Forget about it, people,"Lieutenant Hammer barked. "Get your crap ready. We're about to be on the ground and the clock is running."

"Yes sir,"the others chorused in unison.

As soon as the VTOL touched down, its rear door opened. It felt strange to Shannon, not needing to worry about incoming fire or immediate threats outside. They were on American soil and in the middle of nowhere. On top of that, the LZ had been custom made for them. Moreau Inc. had hired a local company to clear the site.

"What the frag?" Brad wrinkled his nose, shaking his head in disgust.

As the breeze outside blew air into the rear of the VTOL through the open door, Shannon caught a whiff of what Brad had to be smelling. It was rancid, the smell of meat rotting in the burning rays of the sun on a hot summer day. The question was where was it coming from?

"Hold up, people!"Lieutenant Hammer ordered as Brad started to disembark.

"We expecting trouble now all of a sudden?" Deb moved to stand next to Brad by the open door. It was dark outside the jet. Not pitch black but certainly night. All she could see was an excavator. Its running lights were on but dim. At the sight of it, Deb took a step back from the door.

"Well, okay, that's creepy as hell,"Hannah

pointed at the excavator. "I thought the crew the colonel hired was supposed to be out of here before we arrived."

"They were,"Lieutenant Hammer said.

"Then why are that thing's lights on?"Hannah asked.

"Why is it even still here?"Deb added.

"Maybe they're just running late getting out of here,"Shannon offered as an explanation.

"Yeah?" Deb glanced at him. "Then where the hell are they? I don't see anybody out there. Do you?"

"Take it easy,"Lieutenant Hammer ordered them all. "I want lights on, standard defensive formation, on me."

Lieutenant Hammer led them out into the night. The squad began to spread out, the beams of the tactical lights on their rifles sweeping the clearing.

"Lieutenant!"Hannah called out. "I got a dead guy over here!"

"Me too!"Brad shouted.

"Frag,"Lieutenant Hammer muttered as he realized just how deep in it they were.

There were dead men and a few women all over the clearing. They all wore the standard work uniforms of the company Moreau Inc. had hired to get the landing zone ready.

"Well that explains the smell,"Deb said, waving a hand about beneath her nostrils.

"They're all dead." Brad had tensed up and his

eyes kept darting about for any sign of an enemy he could shoot at. "All of them."

"No, really?"Deb glared at him. "Get your crap together, man. This didn't just happen. Whoever did this is likely long gone by now."

"Whoever?"Hannah challenged her. "I think you mean whatever. Look at these poor bastards."

"She's right,"Shannon spoke up, kneeling down to examine the closest body to where he was. "Nobody shot these folks. Something killed them by snapping their bones and slashing them open with claws and teeth. This guy here. . .something even gnawed on him some."

"Holy. . ."Brad stammered. "This is messed the hell up, man!"

"I thought you were all excited about kicking some monster arse,"Deb's tone was harsh.

"That was when he really thought they were just bull,"Lieutenant Hammer said coldly. "Bravado is a coping mechanism for guys like our Brad."

"Sir. . ."Brad started but Lieutenant Hammer held up a hand, silencing him.

The excavator wasn't the only vehicle left at the site. There were several trucks and a bulldozer as well.

All of them ware professional enough to be extremely cautious as they were moving about, checking out the rest of the clearing.

"This guy here looks to have tried to put up a

fight. . . before something tore him in two,"Hannah said shining her light onto the upper half of a man clutching a rifle. It looked as if he had gotten the weapon from the hood of the truck his body was lying next to. The truck's door was open and the lights of its cab were glowing dimly, the battery was dying, furthering the theory that whatever happened here had happened hours or more before the squad's arrival. Hannah moved the beam of her light about the area but the man's lower half just wasn't there to be found.

"Whatever hit these folks, hit them damn hard and damn fast,"Deb said. "These people didn't have a chance in hell."

Shannon nodded in agreement. "Hit them from more than one direction too. Had to have from how these bodies are scattered about. They weren't all trying to run in a single direction."

"Sir,"Hannah waved for Lieutenant Hammer to come to where she was near the truck. "There's something over here you need to see."

Lieutenant Hammer hurried over to see that Hannah was shining the beam of her rifle light onto something on the ground. He blinked. It was a fragging track of some kind, more like a footprint really, and sure as hell not left behind by anything human. Though the shape of the footprint was like a man's and had toes, it was far too large and deep. Whatever made it had to weigh close to half a ton.

"Just what the hell are we dealing with here?"Hannah asked.

"There are a lot more than just that one track,"Shannon piped up, though apparently no one was paying any attention to him. "They're all over this clearing."

Brad came over to look at the print too. "Are you crazy, Hannah? Look at that. You know damn well what we're up against."

"Do we now?"Lieutenant Hammer raised an eyebrow.

"It's freaking Sasquatch, man,"Brad raged. "That's what left that track and you damn well know it. We need to get the hell out of here while we still can."

"Stow that crap right now,"Lieutenant Hammer snapped. "We're not going anywhere. We've got a job to do and we're going to get it done. Is that clear?"

Brad met Lieutenant Hammer's eyes. They stared at each other for a brief moment before Brad's shoulders slumped.

"Yes sir,"Brad answered, his voice low but he was clearly scared out of his fragging mind. It was one thing to go up against other soldiers. It was a completely different thing to find out that a fragging monster was real and you were likely its next target.

"I thought Sasquatch were supposed to be peaceful giants,"Hannah said.

"These ones sure as hell weren't." Deb spat on the ground. "They tore the workers here apart."

"I can see that,"Hannah shot a look at Deb. "I'm not an idiot."

"You're wondering why they did it,"Shannon said. "I'd wager it's because this is their land and they felt threatened. If the creatures are really guarding the relic we're after then maybe that's part of the reason too. They didn't want anyone getting close to it."

"Or maybe the things were just hungry,"Brad huffed.

"You'd better hope they were just hungry,"Hannah said. "Because if it was more than that. . ."

"They could be intelligent,"Deb nodded. "And that would make them even more dangerous than they seem from the looks of this massacre."

"Doesn't matter,"Lieutenant Hammer shined his rifle light on Brad. "We're all gonna get ourselves together and get on with it. Deb, head back into the jet, let Matt and Lance know what's out here. Tell them to seal it up tight, be ready for an emergency lift off, and that we'll be back as soon as we can."

"Yes sir,"Deb nodded and entered the jet.

"As soon as she gets back, we're heading into those woods over there, boys and girls,"Lieutenant Hammer gestured with his rifle light to the north. "That's the direction the thing we're after is supposed to be in and we're going to haul arse to get it. I am sure none of us want to be here any longer than we have to."

The squad was on the move in less than five minutes. Hammer took point himself. Brad brought up the rear with Deb. Hammer didn't trust him back there alone in his current state. All of them were veterans. They'd traveled the globe and had witnessed more than their shares of evil and death, yet today, Brad was suddenly falling apart on them mentally. That was Hammer's take on his current state at least. A single screw up on a gig like this could get everyone killed. He trusted Deb to keep an eye on Brad but still there was only so much she would be able to do if the guy snapped when the crap hit the fan.

There was no real trail through the woods so the going was tough. The team was still using their rifle lights to navigate the way. Hammer made that call because he figured any attempt at stealth was pointless. The monsters that wiped out the work crew called this place home. This was their turf. In one hand, Hammer held his M4 and in the other, the detector he'd been given to locate the relic with. From the pre-mission briefings he knew that not every squad had gotten one. The Sarge's team hadn't. Instead, they'd been given the exact location of the piece of the relic in Africa so there was no need for the tracker.

The tracker crackled and beeped in his hand as

Lieutenant Hammer kept an eye on it. So far, it seemed they were moving in the right direction. He looked up ahead and saw that they were approaching a massive rock that was in the center of some kind of natural clearing. Well, maybe it wasn't natural, Hammer corrected himself. He played his rifle light over the ground around the rock to see that the grass was brown and long dead. There was nothing growing near the rock. Lieutenant Hammer gritted his teeth. Dealing with radiation wasn't a fun thing. He'd done it once before in his career but this time, the rads being put out by this relic were supposed to be harmless. Yeah, right, he thought, grunting in frustration and anger. Now they had yet another reason to get this crap over with as fast as they could.

"Secure this area!"Lieutenant Hammer barked, moving towards the rock. The others spread out, following his order. The tracker was going nuts as he aimed it at the rock. Did that mean the relic was inside the rock or maybe under it? He reached out and placed a hand on the side of the massive rock, frowning. Taking a moment, Lieutenant Hammer snapped the tracker onto his belt and set down his rifle.

"Sir. . ."Hannah said, "We got movement in the trees."

Deb spoke up as well,"Over here too."

"Lieutenant, I think we just might be surrounded, sir,"Shannon added.

"Oh frag, oh frag, oh frag,"Brad was muttering.

"Give me a minute,"Lieutenant Hammer ordered the others, trusting them to hold the line if whatever was out there in the woods rushed their position. Leaning into the huge rock, he braced his feet, and pushed against it with all his strength. The rock moved with such ease that he stumbled and nearly slammed his face directly into it. It had taken effort to move the rock, just not as much as he had expected. The ground was slanted on one side, he saw, to make pushing it aside in that direction easier. Still, no one just leaning on it or even just shoving it a bit would have ever moved it.

Lieutenant Hammer looked down and saw beneath the rock was a small hole. Inside it, something was giving off a faint glow. The rock had been a near perfect means of concealing the relic in plain sight. He didn't like what that implied about the intelligence level of the things that were guarding it.

"Frag me,"Lieutenant Hammer whispered. He reached down and picked up the small piece of metal and examined it. The thing looked like a shard of a broken glass or something, the kind of metal ones that folks drank out of during the time of the Roman Empire. The Sasquatch, or whatever the hell was guarding this thing, must have hid it under the rock to protect it.

At that moment, all hell broke loose. A

cacophony of gunfire hurt his ears as the rest of the squad seemed to open fire. Brad was wailing like a madman, his trigger held tight, hosing the trees with a spray on full auto. Deb and Hannah were firing slower, aiming their shots. Shannon lobbed a grenade into the woods. Seconds later, it detonated. The explosion knocked over a large tree as things, inhuman and feral, cried out in pain from the shrapnel of the blast.

Pocketing the relic, Lieutenant Hammer whirled about, hurrying to join the battle. He fell in beside Deb, who shot him a panicked glance, before returning her attention to the things she was targeting among the trees and deep shadows of the night.

Lieutenant Hammer's breath caught in his throat as he got his first look at one of the things they were up against. The thing stood at least eight feet tall. Its body was covered in thick hair from head to toe, yellow eyes burning with primal rage. Beneath the hair, the Sasquatch, or whatever the hell it was, seemed to be all muscle. He could see that Deb was hitting the thing but her rounds weren't getting much penetration. Honestly, they looked to be just making the thing more angry than it already was.

"Aim for their heads!"Lieutenant Hammer shouted. If it was the density of the creatures' muscles that was protecting them, he hoped their skulls wouldn't be as thick.

With a thunderous roar, one of the beasts made it into their circular firing line. Its hair-covered hands took hold of Brad, lifting him effortlessly, and ripped him in half. Entrails and blood exploded into the air. Hot wetness splashed onto Lieutenant Hammer's face, splattering it with red. He swung the barrel of his M4 around at the monster that had just killed Brad and squeezed the trigger three times in rapid succession. His first shot broke the monster's nose, striking it dead on in the center. His second entered the bestial thing's head through its left eye socket, pulping the yellow orb inside of it. The Sasquatch's head snapped back atop its neck from the impact or maybe the pain. His third shot missed entirely as the wounded beast ducked and charged forward towards him only to stumble and go sprawling out onto the ground. Lieutenant Hammer took a series of quick steps to close the distance between him and the Sasquatch, shoving the barrel of his M4 into its other eye with a wet, squishing sound, before putting another three rounds into its brain. The Sasquatch jerked and thrashed about as he leaped back away from it, dodging its flailing, clawed hands.

"We gotta get out of here!"Shannon yelled.

Lieutenant Hammer knew he was right. If they held their position, they would be overrun. Hell, it was already starting to happen despite the amount of fire they were pouring into the Sasquatch. The things were just too strong and too numerous to be held back. Before he could get out an order for the surviving members of the squad to make a run for the jet, a giant hand grabbed the front of his combat armor and threw him sideways like an angry child casting away a toy. Lieutenant Hammer rolled with the impact when his body smashed into the trunk of the tree he struck as a sickening crunch came from his shoulder. Pain shot through him as bones fractured and folded up inside of it. He landed in the grass at the edge of the clearing where vibrant green met dead, brown blades. Jerking his head up, Lieutenant Hammer saw that his squad had scattered despite him not being able to order them to do it. They were professionals and knew that was the only hope any of them had of making it out of the woods alive. Deb broke one way, Hannah the other. Shannon, though, came running over and yanked him onto his feet.

"Here,"Lieutenant Hammer pulled the relic from his pocket and forced it into Shannon's hand. "Get this out of here or Brad and I will have died for nothing."

Shannon blinked as his words registered. With a quick, sad nod, Shannon left him where he was, sprinting away into the darkness. Lieutenant Hammer had a sawed off, double barrel shotgun in a holster strapped to his leg. Drawing the weapon, he started screaming at the beasts in the woods all around him. "Come on, you bastards! Let's see what you got!"

The sawed off shotgun had the power to blow off a freaking car door. It was his left shoulder that got fragged up so Lieutenant Hammer could still wield the shotgun with his right hand and took aim at the face of an approaching Sasquatch. He emptied both barrels in one single, explosive blast into it. The beast's face seemed to implode as the heavy slugs punched the bones there inward. Dying instantly, the Sasquatch toppled over, clearing the path for the next creature that was already coming his way. Lieutenant Hammer couldn't reload the shotgun with a single hand so he tossed it aside, drawing the .357 Colt Python from the holster on his other hip. The silver of its barrel gleamed in the starlight as he raised the weapon up to fire it.

Needing to buy the others all the time he could, Lieutenant Hammer yelled,"Frag you, you hairy bastards! I got what you want right here."

There were a trio of the hulking beasts around him, two in front and one behind. Lieutenant Hammer spun, dispatching the one behind him first. His .357 thundered twice as he put a pair of gaping holes in the beast's forehead. Whirling back around to face the other beasts, Lieutenant Hammer grunted in pain as the closer of them lashed out with a giant, hair-covered hand. It met his wrist, shattering the bone there. His Colt

Python went flying from his grasp. Lieutenant Hammer's eyes bugged as the beast's other hand closed around his throat. Pain blazed through him as he gasped for breath that wouldn't come. The monster had crushed his windpipe. Lieutenant Hammer kicked and thrashed, vainly trying to break the thing's hold on him. Its grip was like steel though and there was no escaping it.

Lieutenant Hammer died as his head was torn away from the top of his neck by another hairy hand.

Elsewhere among the trees, Shannon was running for his life. His legs pumped beneath him, body covered in sweat born of exhaustion and fear, he pushed himself even harder, picking up his pace. He caught sight of Hannah up ahead of him, off to the right. Shannon shifted his direction to follow in her wake, hoping to overtake her. She must have seen him coming because Hannah skidded to a halt, allowing him to catch up.

"Deb?"he asked.

Hannah shrugged. "Hammer?"

"He's gone,"Shannon answered.

"They're all over the place out here,"Hannah told him.

"I know,"Shannon nodded.

"I've been trying to make contact with Matt and Lance,"Hannah thunked on the side of her helmet. "But the comms are screwed up."

Shannon saw a Sasquatch coming towards

them, bounding through the trees, low lying limbs snapping and breaking off as its shoulders collided with them. Grabbing Hannah, he took off running again, dragging her with him.

"All I can say,"Shannon shouted over the noise the beast was making,"is that they damn well better still be alive and ready to lift off because if not we're utterly fragged."

An M4 blazed away on full auto to the west of them. If they tried to go help her, it only put the two of them at even more risk. Shannon wasn't willing to do that. Hannah outranked him so if she made the call, there wasn't crap he could do about it short of disobeying a direct order.

Glancing over at Hannah as they ran, Shannon could see that she had to be weighing what their course of action should be just as he had done. Based on her expression, Hannah wasn't liking the choices either.

The ability to make the call was taken from them both as the sound of gunfire suddenly drew closer and Deb came darting directly across their path. There were a pair of hulking, hair-covered monsters chasing after her. One of the things noticed them and stopped its pursuit of Deb to attack. Hannah leapt sideways, narrowly avoiding the clawed hand that came her way. Shannon was able to come to a stop and bring up his M4 at the monster. The carbine bucked against his shoulder as he poured half of the weapon's mag into the

Sasquatch. Howling in pain and anger, the thing stumbled backwards. Shannon could see that his bullets hadn't done any real damage to the giant beast. It was more the unexpected violence and suddenness of his attack that drove it into retreat. The Sasquatch righted itself and loosed a roar that seemed to shake the very trees.

"Hannah!"Shannon yelled. "Little help here!"

A spray of bullets tore into the side of the Sasquatch's face, ripping at the flesh of its cheeks and blowing its left eye into a mess of exploding pulp. Seeing the chance to finish the Sasquatch, Shannon opened up on the monster again himself, this time aiming for its head. The Sasquatch finally collapsed.

There was no sign of the other beast that had been with it or Deb. Extending a hand to Hannah, he jerked her up from the ground.

"I'd say we just did what we could for Deb,"Shannon told her as they got moving.

"Agreed!"Hannah snapped.

They ran as close to side by side as possible, racing through the trees, bursting into the manmade clearing where the jet awaited them. Shannon thanked God it was still there. He had half expected either it wouldn't be or that the Sasquatch would have somehow destroyed it. Together, he and Hannah sprinted for the rear of the jet. The door was down as if Matt or Lance had spotted them coming. Their boots clanged against the metal of the ramp and then they were inside. Shannon slammed a hand into the mechanism that shut the door. It rose up from the ground, thudding into place. Whether or not it would hold against an angry Sasquatch, he didn't know. He knew it sure wouldn't hold against an entire pack of them, though. They had to get to the jet in the air. Shannon tried the comm in his helmet.

"Matt! Lance! Get us airborne! Now!"Shannon yelled.

All he got in response was a crackle of static in his ear.

"Shannon!"Hannah got his attention.

He turned his head to see what she saw. A dead Sasquatch lay nearby in a pool of its own blood. Matt's body was pinned to the metal floor beneath it. The pilot's mouth was eternally open in a silent scream. Shannon fought the panic that was rising up within him.

"God help us,"Shannon muttered, managing to hold himself together, as Hannah started for the pilot compartment. The door leading to it was shut and locked. She slapped a hand against it.

"Lance!"Hannah shouted. "If you're in there, open the fragging door!"

With a hiss, the door slid aside, allowing Hannah and Shannon into the pilot compartment. Lance sat in the main pilot seat, pale but very glad to see them.

"Thank God, someone else is alive,"Lance said. "I thought. . . I thought everyone. . .Where's the Lieutenant?"

"We're it,"Hannah told Lance gruffly. "And you need to get us into the air before more of those things try to get in here."

Lance stared at them for a moment longer then nodded briskly. "Right. On it."

The jet rose up into the air, hovering as it turned about as Lance got ready to punch it.

A series of thuds rang out like a violent rain striking a metal roof.

"What the hell is that?"Hannah rasped, rushing forward to look out the window in front of the console where Lance sat.

"Those bastards are throwing fragging rocks at us!"Lance wailed.

"Then get us the hell out of here already!"Hannah snapped.

The VTOL jet's engines roared and it shot northward, disappearing in the night sky, as dozens of Sasquatch howled and roared in the clearing below where it had been.

****

Jason Phisher had been many things in his life - a doctor of various studies, a rich man, a homeless druggie, a bookstore worker but now he was a mercenary. That boggled his mind. The Colonel's offer to join Moreau Inc. had indeed been tempting but it was the feeling that it was what he was supposed to do that made Jason sign up. Another question was why had the Colonel taken him on so quickly? Why sign on a complete stranger? The Colonel and O'Hara had said that their employer insisted he be with them in the quest for the relics they were hired to bring in. Still, was that the only reason? No one knew about his ability. At least not that Jason knew of. Even an idiot could see that he was a man haunted by something and the Colonel was no idiot. For better or worse, Jason had shown them that he could fight. That surely took them by surprise. Bringing him in wasn't exactly easy for O'Hara and Corporal Wiggins. In truth, the two of them shouldn't have succeeded in that. It was further proof of his theory that perhaps he was destined to be where he was right now.

"Jason,"O'Hara's voice returned his attention to the world around him as she reached to touch his hand. "We're here."

He looked out the side window. The VTOL jet had set down next to what appeared to be a very hastily constructed Antarctic outpost. Thrown together quickly or not, the place was more than just a single building. There were three in total. One was sheltering large snow vehicles, another he guessed was home to the makeshift base's generators and comm tower, and the final building was the largest. It was the main part of the base and home to those who manned the place.

Corporal Wiggins sat across from the two of them, smirking at their growing closeness. O'Hara had taken a liking to him though Jason didn't know if it was sincere, an act to control him better on the Colonel's behalf, or worst of all, simply out of pity.

Other than the pilots, there was no one else on the plane aside from the four of them; himself, O'Hara, Wiggins, and the Colonel. None of them were geared up for combat like he'd caught a glimpse of with the members of those leaving aboard the southbound jet that had left right before their own took flight.

"Suit up, people,"Colonel Ringo ordered as Corporal Wiggins jumped out of his seat and started handing out parkas. "It's well below zero out there and the winds are howling."

Jason could hear the wind outside the jet. Glancing through the window as he pulled on the parka Wiggins handed him, a sudden gust of wind blew snow about with such force to make it look like there was a blizzard outside. The moment Wiggins opened the side door, a wave of frigid cold rushed into the jet. It took Jason's breath away for a second from the shock of it. He clutched his parka, pulling it tighter about his chest. O'Hara stepped out first. The Colonel gestured for Jason to go next and followed after him. Wiggins was the last out. Jason had no idea if the pilots would be joining them or not. He didn't even know how long they would be staying themselves.

A man in a heavy parka and trousers above midnight black snow boots emerged from the main building to meet them.

"Welcome, Colonel Ringo! Welcome!"the man beamed.

The Colonel moved ahead of Jason and O'Hara to clasp hands with the man.

"Good to see you, Lev,"the Colonel said.

"Let us get inside before our balls freeze off, eh?"Lev chuckled.

They all entered the building, shrugging their parkas off once they were inside. There were plenty of pegs on both sides of the door to hang them on and they did so.

"Your arrival is later than I expected,"Lev commented.

"We had a last minute situation to deal with,"the Colonel answered, glancing at Jason.

Jason figured he was that situation. Finding him and getting him onboard must not have been part of their original plan. Though O'Hara, and even the Colonel in some ways, had done their best to make him feel welcome, Jason sure didn't feel needed. Beyond Moreau Inc.'s employer insisting him be along, as was the case according to the Colonel, he really didn't feel needed at all. He did have a background in history and lost relics as well as the supernatural and strange occurrences but so far there was no chance for him to apply that knowledge to anything they were doing. The one picture he had been shown hadn't really revealed anything about what they were after except that the three pieces were parts of a greater whole. . . and Moreau Inc. had already known that much. Still, the picture had stirred a powerful sense of dread in him as he had looked at it. Jason felt as if he should know exactly what it was they were after but didn't.

"We've plenty of room for you all!"Lev exclaimed, clapping his hands together. The Russian smiled far too much for Jason's liking. The guy seemed half crazy. "It is only myself, Boris, and Anya here, ya know, yes? These past two months, getting this place ready, was a long and tiresome time. We're all glad to see new faces!"

Lev waved for them to follow him down a corridor that led into a large, open room that was part mess hall and part recreation area from the looks of it. The other two Russians sat at a table playing cards. They looked up as the group entered.

"This is Boris and Anya,"Lev said. "Anya is the grumpy one."

"Watch your mouth,"Anya warned, "or I will cut out your tongue and hang it outside to freeze."

"See?"Lev cackled. "Always such a charmer."

Personality aside, Anya was very much a"charmer". The lady was the epitome of supermodel. Her hair was shoulder length and blonde, eyes a deep blue, and her build was sleek though muscled. She was the kind of woman most men dreamed about.

Boris on the other hand was much the same as Lev, a wide shouldered, tough fellow though his eyes lacked the wildness that Lev's had. He grunted at them in greeting then returned his attention to the cards in his hand.

"As you can see, we've got this place in shape for you, Colonel,"Lev smiled.

"Have you been out to the site?"Colonel Ringo asked.

"But of course,"Lev nodded. "We've not only verified its location but we have Kharkovchankas ready to go for you."

"What is a Kharkovchanka?"Jason whispered to O'Hara.

"Big tank-like vehicle,"she answered. "The limos of the Antarctic."

Jason raised a skeptical eyebrow at that last bit but didn't ask anything more.

"But surely you need some rest from your trip, a chance to get settled in,"Lev said to the Colonel. "As I understand it, there is truly no hurry as you'll be waiting for your other teams to arrive as well, yes?"

That was the first Jason had heard of that. He had no idea that other teams were supposed to come here as well. Jason had assumed that they would all meet back in New York, where Moreau Inc. was located.

"We head out at first light,"Colonel Ringo told Lev. "Not a moment later."

"Not a moment later,"Lev assured the Colonel. "Until then, let us eat, drink, and be merry as they say. It may be cold outside but in here we may celebrate living as we mortal were meant to do, yes?"

Lev opened one of the cabinets mounted on the walls around the room and produced a bottle of Vodka, his smile somehow growing ever brighter.

"I'm in,"Wiggins snatched the bottle from Lev's hand to take a long chug from it.

"Don't overdo it, Corporal,"Colonel Ringo warned and turned back to Lev. "Our quarters?"

"Oh yes! Yes. Anya!"he barked. "Show these fine people to their bunks!"

"But. . ."Anya began to protest.

Lev clapped his hands together. "Time for cards later. Job to do now."

Growling, Anya discarded her hand of cards onto the table in front of Boris and rose to her feet.

"This way,"Anya said, walking briskly from the large room into a second corridor that led out of it.

****

Surprisingly, each of them had their own room. Jason was happy about that when Anya opened the door to his and ushered him on inside. She left without a word, taking Colonel Ringo deeper into the building to his own. O'Hara had remained with Wiggins and the rest of the Russian crew. He doubted that O'Hara was going to drink herself into unconsciousness like Wiggins might, but then Jason didn't know her that well. Either way, he was alone. To have expected O'Hara to come to his quarters with him was too much, despite their growing bond. As much as Jason was happy to be away from the Colonel, his crew, and the Russians who manned this place, he wasn't excited about being alone for the night. There was no doubt that as soon as he closed his eyes, the nightmares were going to come.

With a sigh, Jason looked about the tiny room. Was the space even large enough to truly be called a room? he wondered. It was barely large enough to house the bunk he was meant to sleep on, being not much bigger than a supply closet. There wasn't even a bathroom. That was a communal thing to be shared by them all that was at the other end of the corridor from his quarters.

Sitting down on the edge of his small bed, Jason placed his face down into his hands. Jason realized he was trembling. Tonight was going to be bad but there was nothing to do but go at it head on. He lay back onto the bed and got comfortable, allowing sleep to overtake him.

Jason's eyes flew open inside his dream. The cold was so intense that he screamed. The sound of his voice echoed across the vast and barren landscape of the dream world he had entered. All Jason could see in any direction was white. He sat on snow and ice-covered ground, naked, his arms crossed over his chest, hugging himself tightly. Jason stumbled onto his feet, feeling a presence somewhere close in the white emptiness. Whoever or whatever the presence was, he couldn't see them.

"Hello?"Jason called out.

"So you have come,"an utterly inhuman voice that sounded more like a chorus of voices than a single one chattered in response.

Jason still couldn't see anyone or anything. "I don't even know where I am."

"You are where you are supposed to be, mortal,"the thing he was conversing with answered.

Shaking his head, Jason said,"And just where is that? "

"Jason Phisher,"the voice somehow grew even more inhuman in its sound,"You live between worlds as do we who walks the void. Do you not know this?"

"No I don't!"Jason shouted, anger and frustration welling up to overpower his fear and the pain of the cold around him. "Did you bring me here? Is that what's going on?"

The voice didn't answer. Instead, an area of the brightness shimmered, growing brighter. Out of it walked the thing Jason had met in his nightmares before. It was much larger than a man, a giant towering over him. The green eyes of its over-sized, disproportionate head burned into him like a cold fire. The pincers it had rather than human hands clicked rapidly as did the mandibles over its mouth. Jason stared at the thing in horror and awe. What was it? A demon? An alien? A monster created by his own psyche?

"Why. . .why am I here?"Jason stammered. "Why won't you leave me alone?"

The creature. . . entity. . . whatever it was, looked down at him with glowing, green eyes that burned his soul. It gave no answer however to his questions, continuing to remain silent.

The shimmering portal the thing appeared through was gone. Jason had almost thought to make a run for it in an attempt to escape because there was nothing else but the creature, himself, and the whiteness that lay in every direction.

Without warning, the creature shot forward, closing the distance between them, before he could so much as blink. The pincers of its right hand closed about his throat. They didn't cut into it but rather their sharp edges merely rested against his flesh like a blade waiting to take his life.

"Phisher,"the creature said, its voice echoing both in the endless white and inside his mind,"What you seek. . .it contains power. . More power than a mortal can comprehend."

Jason held perfectly still, terrified to move. "The relic?"he croaked.

The creature laughed though the noise was more akin to a cacophony of crickets chirping. The pincers of its right hand released his throat and with its left, the thing reached out to shove him from his feet. Jason fell backwards, the whiteness absorbing him. It was as if he had fallen into a bottomless sea of nothing. Air rushed by and over him, his arms flailing about vainly. Jason screamed, crying out for help that couldn't possibly hear him or come to his aid.

Jason was still screaming, at the top of his lungs, as he sat bolt upright on his bed. His covers were twisted about him, skin and hair drenched in sweat. The walls and door of his quarters were made of metal, preventing his screams from being heard by anyone else close by. Jason's head snapped back, eyes peering up at the ceiling, as his mind finally broke free from the dream trying to keep him in its clutches. As he fully re-entered the waking world, Jason slumped forward, sucking in huge gulps of breath. He sat there, shaking and trembling, trying to calm himself. The dream had been the worst he'd experienced in a long, long time. Jason rested his face in his hands for a moment and then ran his fingers down along the length of his cheeks before getting to his feet. Staggering into the bathroom, he half fell onto the sink, gripping its sides tightly, looking at his reflection in the mirror above it.

What the bloody, fragging hell was that? Jason wondered. This bit with the creature appearing in his dreams to have a chat with him was really messing with his head. He'd always known his dreams were more than just his subconscious telling him things but this wasn't even that. This felt like something utterly alien reaching into his mind and dominating it. It had to be real but then that would of course mean the creature itself was real too and out there somewhere, maybe waiting for him. He remembered asking it about the relic Moreau Inc. had pretty much kidnapped him to help locate and as he did an image burst into his mind. It burned like fire, pushing all else aside, to reveal itself. In that moment, Jason saw the relic that Moreau Inc. was after, not its pieces but its entirety. And there it was. . . cursing himself for not recognizing it from the pictures of its fragments he'd been shown, Jason released the edges of the sink, rearing a hand back, and smashed a clenched fist into the image of himself in the mirror. The glass broke and shattered. Yelping in pain and flinging drops of red, Jason shook his injured hand. The pain though had finally brought his splintering mind back together.

Jason backed away from the shattered mirror, avoiding looking at it. Instead, he glanced down at his injured hand. The glass had cut him up badly. He was going to need to tend to the damage that been done by his rage. Grabbing a nearby towel, Jason wrapped it tightly around his hand. Jason ignored the pain.

"The Calix Tenebrarum,"Jason muttered. Now he knew exactly what the relic was and why the creature in his dreams was warning him about it. It was a lost item of supposedly unimaginable occult power. The story of the Calix Tenebrarum wasn't complete and aspects of the known parts varied, most of the history being scattered among various arcane tomes and other bits only heard in the oral history surrounding a strange town in Massachusetts. Jason couldn't remember the name of the town exactly but he did recall that it certainly wasn't a place anyone in their right mind would ever want to visit. Some claimed the Chalice could grant immortality much like the Fountain of Youth, others went farther saying it could grant any wish, but the darkest tales spoke of the relic being used to open the door to somewhere far beyond the boundaries of the reality known to humankind and the godlike beings that inhabited those places. It made Jason wonder once more just who Moreau Inc.'s mysterious employer was and just why he wanted the Calix Tenebrarum so badly.

****

It was the middle of the night. Everyone else, except for the few on active duty, were either asleep or drunk out of their minds. Colonel Ringo stood alone at the large observation window, peering out at the landing area used by the base's copters. He watched the CH-53K King Stallion coming in on its approach. Aboard the copter would be the rest of his people as well as a fresh load of fuel and supplies for the outpost. There was an intense storm approaching from the south. Colonel Ringo was glad that the copter had beat it. Had the storm reached the area before its arrival, the copter wouldn't have been able to make it through. That was a danger of operating in the Antarctic. . .the weather. Such a storm could isolate you for days or more. This one was supposed to blow through the area fairly quickly but it still put Colonel Ringo on edge. Unknowns were very dangerous things in the line of work he'd chosen and they could get you killed.

The huge copter touched down. The pilots killed its engine as the side door opened. Colonel Ringo watched his people spilling out. Shannon and Hannah were the first two out. Watkins, aka the Sarge, Rogers, and Artie followed in their wake. Having been in communication with them prior to their arrival, Colonel Ringo was well aware of the losses they had suffered. Those losses pained him greatly. The men and women who died. . .that was on him in a sense. It happened. Colonel Ringo was well aware of that fact, still the day it didn't bother him would be the day he retired.

Colonel Ringo made no move to head out to meet Watkins and the others. He remained at the window, watching them cross the distance between the landing zone and the station through the falling snow. His hands were clasped behind his back and his posture straight, a scowl upon his face. The Sarge and Shannon were carrying two pieces of the relic they had been dispatched to recover with them. All that was left to do in order to finish out their contract with Mr. Than was retrieve the final shard, here in the Antarctic, and deliver them to him. He didn't care for Than at all. The man struck him as an arrogant and selfish bastard. As long as Than's check cleared, though, Colonel Ringo didn't have a real problem with the man. He had worked with A holes in the past and would again too.

Unclasping his hands, Colonel Ringo turned from the window and with a sigh, headed down the corridor to the briefing room where the Sarge and Shannon were supposed to check in. His boots clanged against the metal floor as Colonel Ringo marched in to see the two of them waiting for him. The Sarge had plopped into a chair at the room's table while Shannon was pacing about nervously.

"Sir!"Shannon said as he entered, snapping to attention. The Sarge however continued to recline in his chair and simply gave him a nod.

"It was a bloody mess out there,"the Sarge

grunted. "Lost some good people. Too many."

"I know,"Colonel Ringo nodded.

"Did you know the monsters were real?"Shannon asked him with an almost accusatory tone.

Colonel Ringo shook his head, letting the implication pass. "I did not."

"Who the hell would?"the Sarge huffed. "This job has been so fragging whacko. . ."

"Sergeant,"Colonel Ringo cut him off. "Did you bring the shards of the relic?"

"Of course, sir,"Shannon answered.

"Good. I want them properly secured and a guard posted on them at all times,"Colonel Ringo ordered.

"The crew that put this place together that untrustworthy?"the Sarge asked.

"Let's just say, I think some precautions are needed, Sergeant,"Colonel Ringo said, ending that line of conversation.

"And this last shard. . . it's here?"Shannon frowned.

"It is,"Colonel Ringo looked at them with a stern expression. "I am going to need both of you ready to rock and roll again by tomorrow. I want you with O'Hara when she takes out the Kharkovchanka. The last shard is a few miles south of here. The site has been scouted by the crew here. They didn't report anything out of the ordinary but if the first two sites were guarded by monsters as Mr. Than said they would be you can bet we'll encounter trouble at this one as well. I want us to be prepared this time. No more losses. Is that understood?"

"Yes sir,"Shannon and the Sarge answered in unison.

"That will be all, gentlemen. You're dismissed,"Colonel Ringo gave them a sharp nod.

The Sarge and Shannon left the room, leaving him alone. After they were gone, Colonel Ringo took a seat at the table, drumming his fingers on its top. Watkins was right about this gig being fragged. They would all be better off once it was concluded and their payment was in the bank.

****

The Kharkovchanka was a massive machine. Jason had never seen one in real life before, only on places like the Discovery or History channels. The thing was nearly thirty-five feet long and over a dozen feet wide. He looked up at its thirteen foot tall height in awe. Impressive was the best word to describe the Kharkovchanka. This one looked much sleeker and yet better armored than those Jason saw on TV and the internet. He bet the thing had more horsepower too. Moreau Inc. must have bought it off the Russians somehow and then refit the machine for their own purposes. Jason took a step away from the Kharkovchanka, continuing to stare at the bus/tank hybrid.

"She's a beast, ain't she?"Lev cackled, slapping him on the back.

"I am sure she is,"Jason managed a weak smile. He was still haunted by his dreams of the creature that was likely out there in the snow somewhere waiting for him.

Lieutenant O'Hara, the Sarge, Shannon, and a beautiful but hard looking woman named Artie would be along for the ride as the Kharkovchanka rolled out. Lev was to be its driver being the only one of them fully qualified to do so. The Russian and his people had supposedly taken the massive machine through the snow to wherever it was they were headed a few times before their arrival. Everyone except him was armed. Even Lev had a pistol holstered on his hip. Was the Antarctic nothing more than the Old West with a lot of snow and ice? Jason wondered.

"Everybody aboard!"Lev called out, entering the Kharkovchanka ahead of them.

Lev headed straight for the driver's compartment. Lieutenant O'Hara went with him.

"Jason,"she waved,"You're with us."

The Sarge, Shannon, and Artie remained in the open section of the massive vehicle's interior just outside of the driver's compartment.

Lev thumped his butt down at the controls and fired up the Kharkovchanka's engine. It roared to life with such power the entire vehicle shook for a second. The garage door ahead of it opened as the

Kharkovchanka's tracks dragged it out into the snow.

"The storm's moving in faster than they predicted, eh?"Lev asked no one in particular.

Lieutenant O'Hara didn't bother to respond.

"That's not going to be a problem, is it?"Jason asked.

"Shouldn't be,"Lev smirked. "This beast can handle just about anything. That's what we call her by the way, the Zver."

"Very original,"O'Hara taunted Lev.

"Now, now, Lieutenant,"Lev winked at her. "Let's play nice, eh? I and my people may not be as professional and rigid as you and yours but we do get the job done when it's needed."

O'Hara grunted.

Jason stared out the Zver's forward window. The snow was more than just stuff being blown around now. It was really coming down. He had to squint to see through it to a degree but conditions weren't enough to call it a whiteout. There was nothing to Jason's eyes beyond the front of the Zver but more white.

"E.T.A.?"Jason asked O'Hara.

She gave him the"side eye".

"The site is not far,"Lev answered. "I'd say even with the storm, maybe, half an hour. You in a big hurry, my friend?"

"No,"Jason shook his head. "Not at all."

Glancing around at him, Lev raised an eyebrow

as if surprised by his response.

"You got this?"O'Hara asked the Russian.

"You bet I do,"Lev puffed out his chest. "You two go do whatever you need to. I'll get us where we're going just fine."

O'Hara shoved him to get Jason moving. They exited the driver's compartment leaving Lev alone.

The three soldiers sitting in the main room looked up at them as they entered. Jason had been introduced to all of them since their arrival. The stunning redhead, Artie, was impossible to forget. The big man was simply called the Sarge. And the other. . .Jason couldn't quite remember the guy's name though he thought it might be Shannon. The Sarge and Shannon had been the leaders of the two teams that retrieved the first two shards of the relic. Jason heard it had gone badly and that there were losses, Shannon's team taking the worst.

Artie had a pistol disassembled, spread out on the table she sat at, cleaning the weapon. This portion of the Zver was as much recreational area as it was a mess hall. There were two small tables and half a dozen seats, three toward the room's front and three toward its rear. The Sarge sat with a shotgun resting beside him, chowing down on a bowl of beef stew. Shannon simply returned to staring out a side window, peering into the white of the falling snow.

The Sarge gestured for O'Hara and him to take a seat at the table. The big man stopped shoveling food into his mouth and set his bowl down as he did. "I don't think you're gonna be able to really get it until you see something like we did with your own eyes,"the Sarge told O'Hara.

"He ain't kidding,"Artie agreed. "Monsters. . . no one believes in them. You tell yourself that they can't really exist until. . . you're looking into the eyes of a snarling, half man, half panther creature that wants to tear you apart and eat your insides."

O'Hara shrugged. "If the things can bleed then they can die and that's enough for me."

The Sarge laughed loudly. "That's exactly what I told myself."

"Me too,"Shannon admitted, joining the conversation.

"I think it's what we all do,"Artie glanced around at everyone. "It's like how we cope with the reality of seeing nightmares alive, in flesh and blood bodies, trying to kill us."

"Whatever it takes to get you through, I guess,"Jason commented.

"No,"Artie corrected him. "It's more than that."

Jason met her deep, green eyes with his own about to argue with her but. . .the words wouldn't come.

Lieutenant O'Hara whooped him roughly on the back.

"Jason,"she said, "You're supposed to be our resident expert on all this stuff. What sort of monster do you think we're riding towards right now?"

"Nothing we want to encounter,"he told her,"I promise you that."

"Panther men, Sasquatch, it all seems so fragging insane,"Shannon spoke up. "I imagine Yetis are up next. What else could there be in snow and cold like this?"

"The only Yeti I have ever heard of being in Antarctica are crabs,"O'Hara said.

"Is that a joke?"Jason smirked.

"Sort of,"O'Hara admitted.

"I was going to say most of the cryptids I have heard of in this region are oceanic,"Jason said.

"Spare us the details on them please,"Artie butted in. "Honestly, I'm just ready for this fragging crap to be over with."

"I think we can all agree on that,"the Sarge rumbled.

The Zver lurched under them. The Sarge's bowl of beef stew slid off onto the floor, shattering there. Shannon nearly lost his footing. He shot out a hand to catch himself against the wall of the compartment or would have gone down hard.

"I didn't think we were supposed to be there quite yet,"Jason commented.

"We're not,"Lieutenant O'Hara leaped up from the table and started barking orders. "Everybody, weapons up and be ready. Shannon, watch that window. Artie, go catch out the rear compartments and make sure we haven't picked up any passengers. I'm going to check on Lev."

Jason started to go with her but Lieutenant O'Hara held up a hand, palm out in his direction, shaking her head. "Unh unh,"she ordered. "This time I need you to stay here."

He didn't argue with her. The others sprang into action.

Shannon wiped a hand over the window glass, clearing away the humidity covering it, to peer out into the snow. Jason saw the man's eyes bug.

"Oh frag me,"Shannon's expression was one of pure disgust. "I was fragging joking."

"You're kidding?"Jason said.

"Nope,"Shannon gestured for Jason to come closer. "Take a look out there."

Jason did as he was told. His eyes scanned what he could make out of the hills surrounding the trail that the Zver had been traveling before suddenly coming to a halt. It took him a moment but Jason finally saw what Shannon had. There were humanoid shapes out there so white they blended nearly perfectly into the snow falling around them.

"I see them,"Jason said at last.

"Me too,"the Sarge grumbled.

"I wish I didn't." Shannon readied the M4 he'd snatched up from a nearby seat. "No way to tell how many of those things are out there. Let's hope it's not more than we can handle."

****

Artie made her way towards the rear of the Zver one compartment at a time. She moved slowly, cautiously, not wanting to be taken off guard in case anyone or anything had breached the vehicle already. So far, there was no sign of that having happened. Every room she checked out was empty. Coming to the last section of rooms, Artie found herself staring at the Zver's rear door. It appeared intact and still locked. Artie thought she saw something move, beyond the door, through the small pane of glass that served as its window. Before her mind could even properly register what had happened, the door was ripped outward from its frame. The sound of tearing, bending metal hit her as hard as the blast of cold that came through where the door had been, striking Artie like a punch to her gut. Then the monster was there, coming through, into the Zver at her. The creature was roughly the size of a full grown man. It wore no clothes, covered head to toe in stringy, white hair. Red eyes glowed with primal fury above the sharp teeth that gleamed inside the thing's snarling mouth. The monster was on her before Artie could swing the barrel of her rifle up. White hair-covered fingers clasped the weapon, jerking it from her grasp. Hurling the rifle aside, the monster raised a clawed hand to take a swipe at her. Artie moved with speed that matched the monster's as she drew her pistol, shoving the barrel of her Desert Eagle into its face. The pistol bucked in her hand as she squeezed the trigger. The round from the pistol tore through the monster's skull, leaving a gaping exit wound in its wake as the walls of the compartment were splattered with warm blood and brain matter. The monster's corpse crumpled onto the floor in front of Artie. She took a step back away from it, trying to figure out just what the hell it was that she had just killed. A Yeti? An abominable snowman?

Her attention was pulled back to the rear doorway as Artie heard a chorus of howls outside from somewhere in the snow. She had gotten lucky with this creature and the thought of going up against an entire pack of the things at once and alone didn't appeal to her. The rear door was just. . . gone. There was no hope of closing off the entrance before the creatures out there reached it. The best she could do was retreat into another compartment and lock that door behind her. Whether or not it would hold the monsters out was anybody's guess but based on what she had just seen. . . the odds weren't in the door's favor.

Artie didn't wait for the beasts to reach the door she'd just locked. She needed help and she knew it. Spinning about, Artie ran for the Zver's main room where hopefully the others would be waiting. Her legs pumped beneath her as Artie zigged and zagged from compartment to compartment, closing every door along the way as she went.

Bursting into the Zver's main room, she nearly ran headlong into Jason. He yelped at the sight of her. The barrel of Shannon's M4 and that of the Sarge's pump action shotgun both swung in her direction.

"Don't shoot!"Artie blurted out. "It's me!"

"Damn it, Artie,"Shannon shook his head. "There are creatures out there in the snow."

"Tell me about it." Artie shoved passed Jason, getting closer to Shannon. "They're aboard this thing too."

"How many?"Shannon asked.

"No idea,"Artie answered. "I'd wager at least three or four though from the sound of them."

"Crap,"Shannon growled.

Gunfire erupted from inside the driver's compartment. O'Hara came running out, slamming the door after her.

"Lev is gone,"O'Hara snapped. "Those things out there pulled him straight out through the forward window."

"Frag,"the Sarge grumbled, suddenly taking charge. "We need to find out just what we're dealing with."

"Ain't no way to do that,"Shannon shook his head.

Jason wasn't military but even he could see the choice that lay ahead of them. It came down to hunkering down where they were in the main compartment and holding off the beasts there or taking the battle to the monsters outside and going at them head on. Both ideas had their merits but their own dangers as well. Staying in the compartment left them blind and possibly trapped while rushing out headlong meant they could be overwhelmed and torn to bits.

"I say we stop sitting on our arses and take the fight to those things, show them who they're up against,"the Sarge roared.

"Uh uh, man,"Shannon argued. "We could be walking straight into hell doing that."

"Gentlemen,"O'Hara stopped them. "This isn't a democracy."

"Yes ma'am,"the Sarge and Shannon both said, recognizing her authority.

"So what's it gonna be, ma'am?"the Sarge asked.

"A bit of both,"O'Hara grinned. "Shannon, I want you to stay here with Jason. Hold this compartment and keep him safe at all costs. Meanwhile, the rest of us are going to go pay those bastards a visit."

"Copy that,"Shannon nodded.

O'Hara led everyone but Shannon and Jason out of the compartment towards the rear of the Zver. The beasts that Artie encountered inside the Zver had never pressed farther into the massive vehicle. The group didn't encounter them now as they headed for the rear door either. The things had withdrawn back out into the storm.

The group paused, making sure they were suited up for the cold outside and well stocked on ammo for the weapons they carried before leaving the Zver behind. The Sarge took point as they stepped into the howling wind and falling snow. The rest of the squad spread out behind him into a sort of wedge formation. The creatures would have blended into the snow being blown about by the storm almost perfectly if not for their glowing red eyes. They were everywhere. All around the Zver. As soon as the entire squad was outside, the creatures made their move, charging forward. O'Hara and the others were ready for them though.

The Sarge's shotgun boomed. The heavy slug he fired hammered into the chest of the monster rushing him. Its impact sent the creature flopping over backwards as an explosion of bright red burst outward from where the slug entered. Working the pump of his shotgun to chamber another round, the Sarge switched targets.

Artie had picked up a second Desert Eagle before exiting the Zver. She stood like an Old West gunfighter, blasting away with one pistol and then the other in a flurry of shots. A creature died as Artie put a bullet in its left socket. Another went down screeching in pain as a .50 round blew its groin to shreds of red pulp. As a third sprang at her, both of Artie's pistols barked together and its head exploded in a shower of gore.

Lieutenant O'Hara blazed away with her M4 on full auto, sweeping the weapon back and forth. A trio of the white monsters that were closing in were held at bay and torn up by her spray of fire. As soon as she'd broken the speed of their advance, O'Hara clicked the weapon into semi-auto mode and began to aim more carefully, quickly dispatching the monsters with better aimed shots. As the last of the three creatures fell, her M4 clicked empty. Lieutenant O'Hara yanked the spent magazine out of the weapon and slammed a new one into place.

A creature leaped from atop the Zver at the Sarge. The big man caught a glimpse of it out of the corner of his eye giving him just enough time to heave himself sideways. The creature landed in the snow next to the Sarge, snarling and angry. Lashing out at the big man, who was just as tall as it was, the beast was caught off guard as the Sarge outmaneuvered it. He dodged the swipe of its clawed hand and countered by smashing the butt of his shotgun into the monster's face. Bone crunched as the thing's nose caved inward and blood splattered in the air. Stumbling, the creature wasn't able to right itself before the Sarge managed to swing his shotgun around. With the weapon's barrel now aimed directly at the creature's stomach, the Sarge squeezed the shotgun's trigger. The blast opened up the creature's abdomen, spilling its guts out onto the snow at its feet. The

Sarge worked the shotgun's pump and fired another round into the beast, making damn sure the thing was dead.

Lieutenant O'Hara felt like things were going way too well. The beasts they were engaged with were formidable but she and the others were flat out massacring them. Superior firepower helped of course. Automatic weapons and the .50 caliber rounds of Artie's pistols certainly outmatched the tooth and nail combat the beasts were capable of. Still, there just seemed to be something off about the whole thing to her. A beast charged O'Hara, coming at her from her left side. The second she saw the thing, O'Hara knew she was fragged. There wasn't time to dodge, much less bring her weapon around to bear on it. Gunfire erupted from the Zver's sidedoor. Shannon had flung it open to take out the monster. He was standing there with his M4 raised and its barrel smoking. Relief rushed through O'Hara as she realized Shannon had just saved her arse.

There looked to be only a handful of the white haired monsters remaining as the Sarge hurried to reload his shotgun. Artie had stepped closer to him to provide cover. One of her Desert Eagles cracked as Artie demonstrated just how lethal of a woman she was once more. Entering the skull of a monster that came bounding through the snow at them, the .50 caliber round she'd fired ripped straight through, leaving a gaping exit wound in its wake.

A monster that had been creeping along the length of the Zver, mostly hidden from Shannon's line of sight because of its position, made a grab at him. Shannon screamed as its hand closed on his lower leg. Claws pierced his clothes and flesh alike. With a jerk, the monster yanked Shannon from where he stood in the Zver's side doorway. The back of his head smashed against its frame as he fell. There was a sickening sound of cracking bone as Shannon's skull struck the metal he'd been standing on. His body sprawled out in the snow.

Jason watched Shannon go down in horror, knowing he had to do something or that he would be next. Shannon had forced a pistol into Jason's hands before opening the door to save Lieutenant O'Hara. He made use of it as the beast jumped up into the doorway where Shannon had been standing. The pistol cracked in rapid succession as Jason nearly emptied its entire magazine into the snarling beast. The beast's body bucked and shook as each bullet struck it. The white hair of its upper body now drenched red by its own blood, the beast collapsed, toppling back out of the Zver to thud onto the ground near where Shannon lay.

The Sarge's shotgun thundered a final time and just like that. . .the battle was over. If there were any of the white-haired, man-ape creatures left alive, they'd fled into the storm. All around the Zver were the scattered corpses of the creatures, some bullet riddled, some gutted by powerful shotgun blasts, some even with their heads literally blown off. The snow was stained red with their blood and piles of strewn about, steaming entrails.

"Lieutenant?"Artie asked.

"Everybody back inside,"O'Hara barked.

Jason stared at them all as they entered. He was trembling, barely able to keep a grip on the pistol in his hand. Lieutenant O'Hara reached out and took the pistol from him.

"Good shooting there,"the Sarge grunted, gesturing at the body of the beast Jason had killed.

"It's over, Jason,"O'Hara assured him. "All those things are either dead or run off. Even if there are more out there they won't be coming at us again anytime soon."

"I didn't see Lev's body out there,"Artie commented.

"Don't mean he's alive,"the Sarge said.

"He's dead,"Lieutenant O'Hara told them. "Trust me."

"Then where the frag does that leave us?"the Sarge asked. "I mean, does anyone else know how to drive this thing?"

"We'll manage that,"O'Hara glanced towards the driver's compartment. "We don't have far to go."

"You're forgetting the trip back, ma'am,"the Sarge pointed out.

"Like I said, we'll manage,"O'Hara glared at

him. "Our priority right now is getting our hands on the relic we were sent out here after."

****

Jason had never seen a monster outside of his dreams before. He kept seeing the snarling mouth full of razor-like teeth and rage-filled, red eyes of the Yeti that killed Shannon every time he closed his eyes. There wasn't a lot for him to do as the others got the Zver secured and into motion again. Jason wasn't a mechanic any more than he was a soldier.

The others had settled on O'Hara being the Zver's driver, taking Lev's place. The Sarge was riding shotgun with her in case there were more of the Yeti things around. They had assigned Artie to watch over him. The beautiful redhead sat across from him in the Zver's main room. Both of her Desert Eagles were holstered and she leaned forward, hands clasped between her knees, watching him.

"First time?"she asked.

"What?" Jason blinked.

Artie scowled at him. "You know what I mean."

"No, I don't,"Jason glared at her. "Do you mean killing someone, because I am not sure that thing I shot qualifies as that, or do you mean coming face to face with a bloody monster in real life on such an up close and personal level I could smell the thing's rancid breath?"

"You pick,"Artie chuckled, seemingly trying to break the tension that hung in the air.

Jason couldn't help but find her dark humorous approach to things comforting.

"I guess I am kind of shaken up,"he admitted.

"I would be too in your place,"Artie told him. "Hell, I am still trying to cope with the whole monster crap myself."

"I'm sorry about. . ."Jason started.

Artie waved a hand dismissing what he was trying to say. "Shannon knew the risks. All of us do. There's never any certainty that any of us will be coming home once the crap hits the fan."

"Still. . ."Jason frowned. "I am sorry."

"Yeah,"Artie nodded. "Shannon was a good guy. Lev was too from what I could tell."

Jason didn't know what else to say. A moment of silence lingered between the two of them until Artie finally spoke again.

"So this thing we're after. . .is it worth it?"Artie asked.

"What do you mean by that?"Jason raised an eyebrow.

"This relic, I mean, what the hell is it anyway that someone wants it badly enough to get people killed for?" Artie sighed. "Tell me this isn't all just about money or some rich A hole finishing out his precious collection of ancient oddities."

"It's not,"Jason answered and instantly regretted it. He hadn't really told anyone about his dreams much less their recent revelations. Having opened the door to all that now with how he'd answered, he just stared at Artie, wondering if he could trust her. It likely would've been best to tell Lieutenant O'Hara first. They had at least developed. . . something. . .between them. Before now, Jason and Artie were pretty much complete strangers and mostly still were.

Artie kept her eyes on him, waiting for Jason to continue and explain his answer.

Taking a deep breath, Jason decided to just let it all out.

"The three relics we're after are all pieces of a larger whole. I am sure you knew that much already though. When put back together, they'll make a chalice,"Jason said.

"A chalice?"Artie asked skeptically. "What? Like the Holy Grail?"

"Nothing like the Holy Grail,"Jason shook his head violently. "We're talking about the Calix Tenebrarum."

"The what?"Artie asked.

"It's a powerful, ancient chalice that the stories and legends say could not only grant immortality like the Fountain of Youth by drinking from it but also could make one's wishes realities."

"Like Aladdin's lamp?"Artie smirked.

"No, not exactly. The Chalice doesn't so much grant wishes as give its owner the powers to make their wishes come true,"Jason explained.

"Wow,"Artie seemed impressed yet still disbelieving.

"Here's the catch though,"Jason went on. "The chalice is also supposed to act as a doorway to the worlds beyond ours. Not Heaven and Hell but rather other dimensions inhabited by things that. . . I don't even know how to describe them."

"I've read Lovecraft,"Artie told him,"I think I get what you're saying."

"Yeah! Yeah, that's exactly how to put it,"Jason nodded. "Beings so ancient, alien, and powerful that mankind likely wouldn't survive an encounter with them."

"Extinction level event,"Artie sighed. "Figures. Makes you wonder what our employer wants with the thing."

"Nothing helpful to the rest of humanity I am sure,"Jason said.

"But stuff like magic and aliens from other dimensions aren't real,"Artie argued.

"Would you have said a Yeti was real before today?"Jason pressed her.

"Good point,"Artie admitted. "I guess not."

Artie leaned back in her seat. "So I get the feeling that you believe in all the lore about this Carn-i-whatever."

"I do,"Jason confessed as much to himself as to her. "All my life, I have had dreams. . . feelings. . . that made me think I was crazy. At times, I've even been able to sense and know things that shouldn't have been possible. Those flashes have saved my life too many times for me to remember them all."

"Are you seriously telling me you're like a pre-cog or something?"Artie eyed him.

"Or something, I guess,"Jason nodded.

The Sarge poked his head into the main room,"We're there. It's time to earn our pay."

Jason felt the Zver come to a halt. The Sarge and Lieutenant O'Hara joined them in the main room.

"We've reached the coordinates of where the last bit of this relic is supposed to be,"O'Hara told them all. "There's a fragging cave out there that looks creepier than hell. I am sure it's where we're supposed to head into."

The Sarge grunted in disgusted agreement.

"I want this done by the book, people,"Lieutenant O'Hara ordered. "We've lost more people on this gig already than we have in the last couple of years. No more. Got it?"

Everyone nodded their understanding.

"Jason, I want you with me,"Lieutenant O'Hara told him. "The Sarge will take point and Artie, I want you bringing up the rear. Make sure you're loaded up on ammo and flares, folks. The crap is likely to hit the fan and we need to be ready for it this time when it happens."

****

The storm was dying down. There was still a good deal of snow being blown about but it was nowhere close to the almost whiteout levels from earlier. The Sarge led them out of the Zver. Not far from where Lieutenant O'Hara had parked the massive vehicle was a mound of snow, ice, and rock with an open cave-like mouth leading into its depths. Jason had lost all track of what time it was. He looked at the sky to see that the sun was gone. Whether it was nighttime now or merely eclipsed by the clouds of the storm, Jason didn't know. His heart was pounding inside his chest. As they entered the strange cave Jason felt like the world itself was swallowing them whole. There was no light inside. Lieutenant O'Hara ordered them all to turn on their lights. Artie and the Sarge wore headlights on their helmets. O'Hara, herself, had one mounted on the side of her M4's barrel. Jason was carrying a flashlight in one hand and the pistol Shannon had given him, now reloaded, in the other.

No one knew exactly what was waiting for them at the end of the cave tunnel they'd entered. More Yeti? Some new kind of monster they hadn't encountered yet? Or something far, far worse? Jason shuddered and not from the cold as they marched deeper and deeper into the cave. The tunnel eventually opened up into a wider chamber. The chamber had no other exits than the one they entered through. In its center sat an odd structure composed of stone and ice. It was about the height and width of a normal table though there was no disguising what it had been used for at some long, long passed point in time.

"Tell me that's not a fragging altar,"the Sarge snarled.

"That's exactly what it is,"Jason frowned.

There was an actual path eroded into the stone of the altar where so much blood had run over it. Only God knew how old the thing was. Clearly it predated any real form of human civilization on the other land masses. It was like being in the presence of something. . . something beyond the time of man, Jason thought, but of course there had to have been humans around when the altar was built. Their blood was what had to have flown down its sides.

"Look!"Artie shouted, pointing at the shadowy area of the room behind the altar. A pale glow broke the darkness there. It grew brighter and brighter. The air itself seemed to shimmer and distort as if the fabric of reality itself was being torn open.

Jason saw Artie and the Sarge look to Lieutenant O'Hara for what to do. O'Hara held up a hand signaling not to open fire on the distortion. Every instinct in Jason told him to run. It was like a primal drive kicked in, a fight or flight response in the deepest part of Jason's mind tried to take over and send him running. Jason managed to stay where he was but it took all of his willpower to do so. Glancing around at the others, he could see that they were struggling too. Sweat was beaded on the Sarge's forehead, Artie's face a grimace of determination, and Lieutenant O'Hara had dropped to her knees, eyes fixed on the distortion, knuckles white from the tightness of the grip upon the M4 in her hands.

Out from the distortion stepped the bipedal, insect creature that haunted Jason's nightmares. Knees growing weak, Jason's heart skipped a beat and his breath caught in his throat. It was here. It was real. And its horrid eyes were burning into his soul.

"Phisher,"a cold, inhuman voice buzzed inside Jason's mind. He wondered if the others could hear it too. "You've come at last."

Lieutenant O'Hara, the Sarge, and Artie all held their weapons pointed at the insect thing, waiting on it to make an aggressive move. Jason was surprised they hadn't just started blazing away at the creature. Before the idea occurred to them, Jason forced himself to move forward blocking their line of fire.

"Jason. . ."O'Hara cautioned him.

Shaking his head, he said,"I know this thing."

Lieutenant O'Hara's mouth fell open. The Sarge and Artie looked equally as shocked.

"I'm here,"Jason said to the creature, holstering his pistol and extending his arms out to his sides in a gesture of peace.

"I have what you seek,"the creature spoke into his mind again. "Here."

The top of the altar appeared to melt and from the churning magma of the heated rock arose the third and final piece of the Calix Tenebrarum. The altar became solid again beneath the piece as it laid upon the rock, steam hissing upwards.

"This is your destiny,"the insect thing buzzed. Jason could see that this time the others heard the buzzing voice of the creature too. Leaning forward, its wings fluttering, the insect thing moved one of its pincer-like hands over the piece of the Calix Tenebrarum. The steam stopped. Jason could see that the piece was cool now and should be safe to touch.

"Come. Take it,"the insect thing urged Jason.

"Why?"Jason asked. "Why give it to me?"

"You know why,"the insect thing told him. "The other who seeks this will break the worlds. That can not be allowed to happen. With you, this will be safe."

Jason stared at the creature. He didn't want the final piece. He didn't want any of the insanity that was his life. All he wanted was to be normal. . . something that his life had never been. Still, there was no choice but to do as the thing asked. He moved forward and reached out for the piece of the ancient relic that was being presented to him. The hair on Jason's arms prickled and stood up as he touched it. Energy coursed through his body and into him. Jason could feel its evil. His stomach turned and the world spun before his eyes. A supernatural chill left Jason shivering as he lifted the relic from the altar.

"Farewell, Phisher,"the insect spoke into his mind and then was gone. In a flash of light, the insect creature vanished. Jason assumed that it had returned to whatever other world or dream space that it resided in but for all he knew the being had simply ceased to exist, its purpose fulfilled.

"Hey man,"the Sarge called to him. The big man had shrugged off his backpack and held it open, extended towards him. "Put that thing in here."

Jason, unable to even really think for himself in the moment, did as he was told, dropping the relic into the backpack. It felt like an unimaginable weight was taken off of him. As soon as the relic was out of his hands, Jason slumped to the floor of the room, collapsing onto his knees.

Lieutenant O'Hara rushed over, kneeling next to him.

"Are you okay?"she asked, sincere concern in her voice.

Jason managed to nod.

"Artie, help him up,"Lieutenant O'Hara barked. "We need to get that thing back to the Colonel A.S.A.P."

"Couldn't agree with you more,"Artie

commented as she helped Jason to his feet.

His legs were shaky and his mind still reeling but with Artie helping to support his weight, Jason was able to steady himself.

The room around them begin to rumble and shake.

"Oh fragging hell,"the Sarge raged.

"I think this place is about to come down around us,"Artie said.

"Then let's not waste any more time,"Lieutenant O'Hara snapped. "Run for it!"

The group raced back along the cave, exiting its mouth out into the snow seconds before the mound they'd been inside crashed inward upon itself.

"That was too damn close,"the Sarge grumbled.

"Uh. . ."Artie said, eyes wide.

Jason looked to see that they were surrounded. The Yeti creatures were everywhere. Their red eyes glowed amid the blowing snow. The winds had settled and the storm was over. They made no move to attack, standing motionless, like statues. If Jason hadn't been able to see their breath in the cold, he'd have thought the things were dead and frozen in place.

"Lieutenant. . ."the Sarge whispered, looking to O'Hara.

"Don't engage them,"Jason answered before she could.

O'Hara's head snapped around in his direction.

Jason didn't know why but his gut told him that

the creatures weren't there to harm them. He could feel through the supernatural sense that haunted him most of his life that the things had lost their purpose. . . their drive. His eyes met O'Hara's. The two stared at each other for a moment.

By the time Lieutenant O'Hara returned her gaze to the monsters, they were leaving. Each and every one of the things simply turned about and vanished into the snow.

"What the Hell?"the Sarge asked.

"They have nothing left to protect,"Jason told him. "The relic is ours now and they seem to know and accept that."

"I ain't arguing,"Artie remarked, clearly happy not to be in another battle with the creatures.

Lieutenant O'Hara motioned for the others to get moving towards the Zver.

****

Colonel Ringo stood at the base's observation window, watching the Zver roll in. The huge vehicle had been damaged. He saw that its rear door was gone and that its sides were scarred by what appeared to be claw marks. Once it was safely inside the base's garage, Colonel Ringo let out a sigh of relief. God only knew how many more of his people were dead but at least some of them had survived. Turning away from the window, Colonel Ringo walked through the corridors of the base to the briefing room where his people in the Zver had been ordered to report to upon their return. He took his time, moving slowly, giving them time to get there ahead of him. When Colonel Ringo entered the briefing room, Lieutenant O'Hara, the Sarge, Artie, and Dr. Jason Phisher were there waiting on him. They were all seated at the table in its center except for Artie. She leaned against the far wall.

"The others?"Colonel Ringo asked, already knowing the answer.

"Dead, sir,"Lieutenant O'Hara answered, frowning.

Colonel Ringo took a seat at the head of the table. "Were you able to obtain the objective?"

Lieutenant O'Hara nodded.

The Sarge lifted a backpack that sat on the floor next to his chair onto the table. Opening it, the big man carefully shook the relic from the pack out. It clanked onto the table top.

"Careful,"Lieutenant O'Hara cautioned.

"Sorry,"the Sarge said, "But I ain't touching that thing. Besides, it's been around for God knows how long. I'd say the thing is pretty damn tough."

"He's right,"Jason spoke up. "That thing is said to be indestructible."

"Nothing is indestructible,"Colonel Ringo commented.

"I wouldn't be so sure of that, sir,"Lieutenant O'Hara said. "A few days ago, none of us would have believed in monsters either."

"We've got all three pieces of the damn thing now,"the Sarge growled.

"And we paid dearly for them,"Artie said.

"That we did,"Colonel Ringo agreed. "Too damn high."

"So where do we go from here?"Lieutenant O'Hara leaned forward.

"We get this thing to our employer, get paid, and wash our hands of this whole fragging mess." Colonel Ringo stood up, towering over those seated at the table. "I think we're all ready to be done with this crap. The storm has passed through and is gone. We should be able to fly out later today."

"Hold on a second,"Jason said as everyone else was getting up from their seats too. "You're not thinking this through."

"What?"Colonel Ringo was clearly put off by Jason speaking up.

"This relic,"Jason said. "Remember, you brought me here because I know it."

"And your point?"Colonel Ringo snapped.

"I am saying this thing is supposed to hold an incredible amount of power." Jason stared up at the Colonel. "Can you trust your employer with it if that's true?"

"That's not our concern, Dr. Phisher,"Colonel Ringo shook his head, dismissing his concern. "Our job is to get it to him, nothing more."

"Maybe it should be,"Jason countered. "If this

thing can. . ."

Colonel Ringo cut him off. "That will be quite enough, Doctor."

Jason could see that if he pressed Colonel Ringo more on the subject that things wouldn't go well for him. The three pieces of the relic were gathered and ready to be delivered. All the Colonel could think about was likely the paycheck that was about to be his. Jason had nowhere else to go and nothing ahead of him aside from the place he was promised in the Colonel's organization.

The door to the briefing room was flung open. Skittish as they were from all the hell they'd been through, Artie, the Sarge, and even Lieutenant O'Hara all aimed weapons at the woman who came through it.

"Nyet! Do not shoot!"Anya squealed.

"People! Let's all calm down,"Colonel Ringo chided the others who lowered their guns, though his own hand rested on the butt of the pistol holstered on his hip.

Jason knew that Anya and Boris had to be taking Lev's death hard.

"What is it, Anya?"Colonel Ringo asked the blonde Russian.

"Sir. . .There's. . ."Anya stammered.

"Spit it out,"Colonel Ringo ordered.

"There's a copter inbound, sir,"Anya managed to get out.

The others all looked at each other then back at the Colonel.

"That's impossible,"Colonel Ringo barked.

"It's not answering on the radio, sir,"Anya went on. "No transponder signal either."

"Oh crap,"the Sarge scowled.

"Double cross?"Artie asked.

"Maybe our employer is just a tad over eager to get his hands on the prize we collected for him,"Lieutenant O'Hara said, though Jason couldn't tell if she was trying to reassure them or herself that the crap wasn't about to hit the fan.

Boris appeared in the doorway behind Anya. The burly Russian's expression was grim.

"They've landed,"Boris' deep voice boomed.

"Colonel?"Lieutenant O'Hara asked.

"Boris, Anya, if you would please meet our uninvited guests and escort them here,"Colonel Ringo told them.

"Phisher, you're with me,"Colonel Ringo said. "Everyone else, stay here and be ready for trouble if it comes."

"Yes sir,"Lieutenant O'Hara nodded.

Jason followed the Colonel out of the room. Boris and Anya had already departed ahead of them. Colonel Ringo led Jason to the observation window that looked out onto the helicopter landing area.

"His name is Dixon Than,"Colonel Ringo informed him. "He's one of those richer than a small god A holes."

They watched as several men poured out of the copter's side door. All of them wore white, Arctic gear and were armed to the teeth. Jason counted eight of them. They spread out creating a perimeter around the copter before another man dressed in a black business suit. The man seemed oblivious to the cold and the wind outside had stopped blowing. After he'd disembarked from the copter another two armed men in white emerged behind him.

"Than?"Jason frowned. "I feel like I've heard that name."

"You may have,"Colonel Ringo nodded. "The guy has got his fingers in everything from media to tech to social foundations."

"You know his name means death in ancient Greek,"Jason said.

"I didn't but that fits the bastard,"Colonel Ringo shrugged. "And he's sure as hell got us outnumbered. Nine to seven even if you count the crazy Russians as being on our side."

"They aren't?"Jason asked.

"They're independent contractors brought in just for this job,"Colonel Ringo shrugged again. "They could go either way if the crap hits the fan so no, we can't count on them."

"Know who the guys with him are?"Jason expected Colonel Ringo to answer yes and the Colonel didn't let him down.

"Yeah, those creeps are his personal bodyguards,"Colonel Ringo looked worried to Jason. That wasn't a good sign for their survival if Mr. Than had arrived with ill intentions.

The two of them returned to the briefing room to await the arrival of Mr. Than and his guardsmen.

There was no sound of gunfire so Jason figured that Anya and Boris at least hadn't been gunned down by Than's people. Of course, as the Colonel had pointed out, the Russians were mostly neutral.

****

Jason, Colonel Ringo, Lieutenant O'Hara, the Sarge, and Artie all stood facing the briefing room's entrance as Than's men entered. No one said anything. The soldiers in white broke up into two groups of three on each side of the door before Mr. Than himself finally came through it. That left two of his men unaccounted for, out there in the base somewhere, perhaps holding the Russians at gunpoint for all Jason knew.

"Colonel,"Mr. Than smiled. "I trust you have the items I hired you to find."

"I do,"Colonel Ringo met Than's smile with an expression as hard as stone. "They didn't come cheap though."

"Nor did I expect they would,"Mr. Than smirked. "That is after all why I am paying you so much, Colonel."

Another of Than's men came into the briefing

room carrying a large suitcase. He set it down on the top of the table and opened the case before backing away from it. Inside was more money than Jason had ever seen in his entire life.

"There's two point four million in the case, Colonel,"Mr. Than said. "I've also transferred another eight in Moreau Inc.'s account. Feel free to check that if you'd like."

"That's more than we agreed on,"the Colonel admitted.

"You've done fine work, Colonel,"Mr. Than chuckled. "We both know the task I set for you was not an easy one."

An awkward moment of silence passed before anyone spoke again. It was Mr. Than who broke that silence.

"Now if you would be so kind, I'd like the relics you gathered for me." Mr. Than steepled the fingertips of his hands in front of his chest.

"Right,"Colonel Ringo nodded. "Of course."

The Colonel motioned to the Sarge and Artie. They approached the table. The Sarge dumped the piece they'd just gotten from his backpack out. It struck the table with a loud thud making all of them, especially Mr. Than, flinch. On the shelf near where Artie had been standing was a case much like the one Mr. Than's men brought in though smaller. Artie had picked it up and carried it to the table. She sat it down, flipping the case open. Inside were the other parts of the Calix

Tenebrarum. Having delivered what they needed to, both the Sarge and Artie backed away from the table.

Mr. Than sucked in a slow, deep breath. Jason could see the excitement at the presence of the relics though Than was clearly trying to hide it.

"Again, Colonel, allow me to congratulate you and yours on a job well done,"Mr. Than said. "You may take your money and leave now."

"Colonel,"Jason spoke up in the hope of getting Colonel Ringo to think about what he was doing.

"Ah, Dr. Phisher,"Mr. Than purred. "I wondered if perhaps you might present a problem at this meeting."

"Jason's just a bit overtaxed, Mr. Than,"Lieutenant O'Hara butted in. "We've all been through a lot getting this job done and as you know, he's not a professional like the rest of us."

"Most assuredly not,"Mr. Than agreed, "But he was the key to acquiring the final shard of the chalice. Without him, it would not have been possible."

"Is that so?"Colonel Ringo huffed, insulted by the implication that he and his couldn't have gotten the job done on their own.

"There's no slight to your pride, Colonel,"Mr. Than told him. "There were mystical forces at play which simply required Dr. Phisher's presence."

"I am right here,"Jason snarled.

"Indeed you are, Doctor,"Mr. Than laughed.

"You can't let him have the relics,"Jason took a step towards the table. The guns of the soldiers in white all came up, barrel aimed at him. In response, the Sarge, Artie, and Lieutenant O'Hara raised theirs.

"Whoa!"Colonel Ringo shouted, reaching out to shove the barrel of Lieutenant O'Hara's rifle down. "Hold on now, people. Let's not do something we're all going to regret here."

"You have to listen to me, Colonel,"Jason pleaded. "If you give him. . ."

Colonel Ringo whirled on Jason. "Will you fragging shut up already or do I have to close your mouth for you?"

Jason recoiled from the fury in Colonel Ringo's eyes.

"A deal is a deal as they say, yes?"Mr. Than cackled.

"Yes,"Colonel Ringo nodded at Mr. Than. "It certainly is."

"Can't you see he's evil?"Jason shrieked. "He'll destroy the world!"

Before anyone could react, lunging forward, Jason swept up the three pieces of the Calix Tenebrarum. As he touched them and the pieces touched one another, something happened. Light flared as if there was sun going super nova inside the room.

"Stop!"Mr. Than screamed, lunging forward himself but it was too late.

Jason stood, strong and tall, beside the table. The pieces of the Calix Tenebrarum were gone, merged with his body. They'd been absorbed into him from the look of things. Jason's eyes glowed an eerie shade of purple.

"Oh yes,"Jason said in a voice that sounded like a chorus of angels, "That's much better."

"Kill him!"Mr. Than wailed at his men.

"No!"Lieutenant O'Hara shouted. Jerking up her M4, she let loose at the soldiers in white, cutting one of them down. Patches of red blossomed on the man's uniform as her bullets ripped into his chest and he reeled backwards into the wall. The other soldiers were all firing at Jason.

The Sarge tackled Lieutenant O'Hara, taking her to the floor behind a desk at the rear of the room.

"Stay the hell down,"the big man roared.

Artie dove for cover too, joining them behind it.

Colonel Ringo remained close to where he was, moving just enough to get out of the soldiers' line of fire while still facing Mr. Than and his soldiers, pistol drawn and aimed in their direction.

Bullets struck Jason, knocking him about, making him dance like a puppet on the strings of a deranged master. Blood splattered from his many wounds. The soldiers kept firing until their weapons were emptied. . .and yet, Jason still stood on his feet. A wicked grin formed on Jason's lips below his glowing purple eyes.

"Jason!"Lieutenant O'Hara yelled from where the Sarge held her tight behind the desk at the rear of the room.

The soldiers were gawking at him, stunned and terrified that Jason was not only still alive but healing right in front of their eyes.

Mr. Than's icy composure was shattered. He, too, looked scared. Waving his hands, fingers twisting in intricate gestures, Mr. Than began chanting in a language that was long dead.

"Uh uh,"Jason chided. "We'll have none of that."

With a flick of his right hand in Mr. Than's direction, Jason sent him flying. One of Than's men caught him or he would have crashed into the wall next to the room's door with such force that his bones would have shattered.

Two of the soldiers in white rushed forward trying to get a hold of Jason and restrain him. Jason was faster. His hands caught each of the men by the throat, lifting them effortlessly from the floor. They struggled and kicked against his grasp. Crushing their throats so the heads of the soldiers bent at unnatural angles and their bodies went limp, Jason flung them aside. Several of the other soldiers had managed to get their weapons reloaded. They started blasting away at him again. Jason dove into their ranks with a mad glee. The flesh of his own hands split open in explosions of blood as pincers erupted outward from inside his wrists to take their place. The pincers at the end of his right arm snipped another soldier's face in two like razor blades closing upon it. The pincers of his left relieved a different soldier of his manhood. The remaining soldiers in white fought back. One drew a pistol, discharging it point blank into the center of Jason's forehead. Head snapping back atop of his neck, Jason staggered. The glow of his purple eyes didn't even dim, though if anything it grew brighter.

"Enough!"Jason bellowed like a roll of thunder, flinging his arms outward to each side. As he did so, each and every one of the soldiers that were still alive blew apart, chunks of bloody meat spinning through the air. The mess of them splashed in patches all around the room.

"Nolite in nomine dei!"Mr. Than wailed, a hand extended towards Jason.

"Little man,"Jason turned his purple eyes on Mr. Than. "Do you truly believe yourself capable of challenging me?"

Mr. Than was on his feet again. If he was shaken by what Jason had done to his men, Than didn't show it. His forehead was drenched with sweat, though, and his eyes focused on Jason with fierce determination.

"Ad Inferos!"Mr. Than raged.

Jason opened his mouth and it continued to open and open and open. Through Jason's lips came a new head, insectoid and utterly inhuman.

His hands came up to grab the stretched rolls of flesh that slid down the exoskeleton of Jason's new neck. They took hold of it and with a powerful yank ripped the rest of it and Jason's shirt alike, exposing the upper half of his new body. Large, black wings unfolded from Jason's new back, flapping behind him.

Advancing on Mr. Than faster than the human eye could follow, the pincers of the thing that was once Jason clamped down onto his shoulders. Mr. Than howled in pain, his skin cut open as if by a pair of scissors where Jason clutched him. From beneath the mandibles that covered Jason's new mouth a proboscis shot out, driving itself into Mr. Than's forehead. It pierced the bone of his skull. Horrid, wet, sucking noises followed as Than's eyes rolled up to show only whites.

"Okay, people,"Colonel Ringo roared. "Let's take this bastard out!"

Leveling the barrel of his pistol at the thing which had been Jason, Colonel Ringo squeezed the trigger in rapid succession. They came to a halt in the air just short of hitting the insect thing's body. Though its new eyes were nothing like Jason's had been, they continued to give off a purple glow. The thing shook its head in the negative and the bullets, frozen in the air, were flung back towards Colonel Ringo at near supersonic speed. They tore through his flesh as if it were tissue paper, spraying his blood and entrails out through the exit wounds they left in their wake. Colonel Ringo's ravaged remains toppled to the floor.

Artie attacked next. She jumped up from the deck, charging the Jason-thing, firing Desert Eagles thundering. .50 caliber rounds cracked his exoskeleton, making the insect creature stagger. She'd caught it off guard and pressed her attack. Her aim shifted from its chest to its head. One of her shots clipped the side of its skull, another ruptured the mass that was the thing's left eye. A furious chatter arose from the Jason-thing. A beam of pure, purple energy flashed from its remaining eye, striking Artie. Skin seared from her bones; Artie died instantly.

The Sarge and Lieutenant O'Hara were the only ones left alive in the room with the monster.

"We gotta do something,"the Sarge whispered.

"What?"Lieutenant O'Hara pressed the big man.

"Artie hurt that thing,"the Sarge pointed out. "If it can be hurt, maybe it can die."

Lieutenant O'Hara put a hand on him,"Don't."

"Like I said,"the Sarge gave her a sad glance,"we gotta try."

Leaping to his feet the Sarge worked the pump of his shotgun, chambering a round.

"Hey, pretty boy,"the Sarge called out to the insect creature.

Emitting a sort of buzzing sound, the creature turned towards him.

The Sarge's shotgun boomed. The heavy slug it

fired slammed into the monster's chest. The shot didn't break through the exoskeleton there but did crack it. The bug-thing screeched. Chambering another round, the Sarge took aim at the monster's head. As he fired, though, the thing lunged forward. His shot whizzed by its skull without making contact. The monster plowed into him, driving the Sarge into the metal wall behind the desk. The big man was smashed against it, his spine snapping and ribs caving inward. Blood rose up from inside the Sarge, spraying from his mouth. The creature released the big man, letting the Sarge drop to the floor at its feet.

Lieutenant O'Hara stared up at the monster.

"Jason," she begged. "Please."

The creature paid no attention to her whatsoever, instead turning its head upwards.

"Jason," O'Hara whimpered again.

"Let the veils be parted," the insect thing said in a buzzing voice and then squealed.

Lieutenant O'Hara's head popped like an overripe melon, exploding, as the sky itself was torn asunder.

Somewhere beyond the veil of reality, in a realm of writhing tentacles, something ancient beyond the comprehension of mankind answered it with a shriek that shook the Earth. Billions of voices cried out around the globe as their sanity was taken from them at the sound of it.

END

Author Bio

Eric S Brown is the author of numerous book series including the Bigfoot War series, the Psi-Mechs Inc. series, the Kaiju Apocalypse series (with Jason Cordova), the Crypto-Squad series (with Jason Brannon), the Homeworld series (With Tony Faville and Jason Cordova), the Jack Bunny Bam series, and the A Pack of Wolves series. Some of his stand alone books include War of the Worlds plus Blood Guts and Zombies, Casper Alamo (with Jason Brannon), Sasquatch Island, Day of the Sasquatch, Bigfoot, Crashed, World War of the Dead, Last Stand in a Dead Land, Sasquatch Lake, Kaiju Armageddon, Megalodon, Megalodon Apocalypse, Kraken, Alien Battalion, The Last Fleet, and From the Snow They Came to name only a few. His short fiction has been published hundreds of times in the small press in beyond including markets like the Onward Drake and Black Tide Rising anthologies from Baen Books, the Grantville Gazette, the SNAFU Military horror anthology series, and Walmart World magazine. He has done the novelizations for such films as Boggy Creek: The Legend is True (Studio 3 Entertainment) and The Bloody Rage of Bigfoot (Great Lake films). The first book of his Bigfoot War series was adapted into a feature film by

Origin Releasing in 2014. Werewolf Massacre at Hell's Gate was the second of his books to be adapted into film in 2015. Major Japanese publisher, Takeshobo, bought the reprint rights to his Kaiju Apocalypse series (with Jason Cordova) and the mass market, Japanese language version was released in late 2017. Ring of Fire Press has released a collected edition of his Monster Society stories (set in the New York Times Best-selling world of Eric Flint's 1632). In addition to his fiction, Eric also writes an award-winning comic book news column entitled "Comics in a Flash" as well a pop culture column for Altered Reality Magazine. Eric lives in North Carolina with his wife and two children where he continues to write tales of the hungry dead, blazing guns, and the things that lurk in the woods.

Check out other great
Cryptid Novels!

J.H. Moncrieff
RETURN TO DYATLOV PASS

In 1959, nine Russian students set off on a skiing expedition in the Ural Mountains. Their mutilated bodies were discovered weeks later. Their bizarre and unexplained deaths are one of the most enduring true mysteries of our time. Nearly sixty years later, podcast host Nat McPherson ventures into the same mountains with her team, determined to finally solve the mystery of the Dyatlov Pass incident. Her plans are thwarted on the first night, when two trackers from her group are brutally slaughtered. The team's guide, a superstitious man from a neighboring village, blames the killings on yetis, but no one believes him. As members of Nat's team die one by one, she must figure out if there's a murderer in their midst—or something even worse—before history repeats itself and her group becomes another casualty of the infamous Dead Mountain.

Gerry Griffiths
CRYPTID ZOO

As a child, rare and unusual animals, especially cryptid creatures, always fascinated Carter Wilde. Now that he's an eccentric billionaire and runs the largest conglomerate of high-tech companies all over the world, he can finally achieve his wildest dream of building the most incredible theme park ever conceived on the planet... CRYPTID ZOO. Even though there have been apparent problems with the project, Wilde still decides to send some of his marketing employees and their families on a forced vacation to assess the theme park in preparation for Opening Day. Nick Wells and his family are some of those chosen and are about to embark on what will become the most terror-filled weekend of their lives—praying they survive. STEP RIGHT UP AND GET YOUR FREE PASS... TO CRYPTID ZOO

Check out other great

Cryptid Novels!

Hunter Shea

LOCH NESS REVENGE

Deep in the murky waters of Loch Ness, the creature known as Nessie has returned. Twins Natalie and Austin McQueen watched in horror as their parents were devoured by the world's most infamous lake monster. Two decades later, it's their turn to hunt the legend. But what lurks in the Loch is not what they expected. Nessie is devouring everything in and around the Loch, and it's not alone. Hell has come to the Scottish Highlands. In a fierce battle between man and monster, the world may never be the same. Praise for THEY RISE : "Outrageous, balls to the wall...made me yearn for 3D glasses and a tub of popcorn, extra butter!" – The Eyes of Madness "A fast-paced, gore-heavy splatter fest of sharksploitation." The Werd "A rocket paced horror story. I enjoyed the hell out of this book." Shotgun Logic Reviews

C.G. Mosley

BAKER COUNTY BIGFOOT CHRONICLE

Marie Bledsoe only wants her missing brother Kurt back. She'll stop at nothing to make it happen and, with the help of Kurt's friend Tony, along with Sheriff Ray Cochran, Marie embarks on a terrifying journey deep into the belly of the mysterious Walker Laboratory to find him. However, what she and her companions find lurking in the laboratory basement is beyond comprehension. There are cryptids from the forest being held captive there and something...else. Enjoy this suspenseful tale from the mind of C.G. Mosley, author of Wood Ape. Welcome back to Baker County, a place where monsters do lurk in the night!

Check out other great
Cryptid Novels!

P.K. Hawkins
THE CRYPTID FILES

Fresh out of the academy with top marks, Agent Bradley Tennyson is expecting to have the pick of cases and investigations throughout the country. So he's shocked when instead he is assigned as the new partner to "The Crag," an agent well past his prime. He thinks the assignment is a punishment. It's anything but.Agent George Crag has been doing this job for far longer than most, and he knows what skeletons his bosses have in the closet and where the bodies are buried. He has pretty much free reign to pick his cases, and he knows exactly which one he wants to use to break in his new young partner: the disappearance and murder of a couple of college kids in a remote mountain town.Tennyson doesn't realize it, but Crag is about to introduce him to a world he never believed existed: The Cryptid Files, a world of strange monsters roaming in the night. Because these murders have been going on for a long time, and evidence is mounting that the murderer may just in fact be the legendary Bigfoot.

Gerry Griffiths
DOWN FROM BEAST MOUNTAIN

A beast with a grudge has come down from the mountain to terrorize the townsfolk of Porterville. The once sleepy town is suddenly wide awake. Sheriff Abel McGuire and game warden Grant Tanner frantically investigate one brutal slaying after another as they follow the blood trail they hope will eventually lead to the monstrous killer. But they better hurry and stop the carnage before the census taker has to come out and change the population sign on the edge of town to ZERO.

www.ingramcontent.com/pod-product-compliance
Lightning Source LLC
Chambersburg PA
CBHW061250170626
46809CB00007B/2925